JENNA'S CHRISTMAS WISH

Debra Parmley

DCL Publications, LLC

www.thedarkcastlelords.com

© 2015 Debra Parmley

All rights reserved

First Edition November 2015

DCL Publications
1033 Plymouth Dr.
Grafton, OH 44044

ISBN 978-0-9964959-8-1

No part of this book may be reproduced or transmitted in any form by any means, electronic or mechanical, including photocopying, recording, or by any information and storage retrieval system, without permission in writing from the copyright owner.

This is a work of fiction. Names, characters, places and incidents are the product of the author's imagination, and any resemblance to any actual persons, living or dead, events, or locales, is entirely coincidental.

Cover design by Lynn Hubbard

PUBLISHED IN THE UNITED STATES OF AMERICA

Dedicated to every girl who has dreamed of a happy ever after with her real life hero and every good guy who behaves like a hero.

Heroes do exist and we know them by their deeds.

Thank you John Antorino for the inspiration for this story and for the work you do for cancer patients and thank you for appearing on my cover. Thank you to Destiny Blaine for the wonderful writers weekend in the mountains and my first experience with wolves. That was one night I will never forget.

My thanks and appreciation to Tina Taran my first reader. My thanks and appreciation to the Dark Castle Lords family, especially Lady Pamela Seres my publisher, Lady Jean Watkins my editor, and my cover artist Lady Lynn Hubbard.

Infinite love and gratitude to you, my readers. May you be a hero and may you find your happy ever after with the hero of your dreams.

Table of Contents

CHAPTER ONE

Why did everything have to be so cold and barren this time of year? If only there was a way of finding warmth, happiness and joy again. Less than three weeks until Christmas. Not enough time.

Jenna gave up hope of having a merry Christmas as she drove through the mountains of east Tennessee, taking in the cold white snow, the black silhouettes of trees and the wintery sky as the sun faded behind the tree lines.

Here and there, through the trees, she caught glimpses of houses with Christmas lights on them. The multicolored blinking lights and the big red Santa in one yard should have cheered her up but didn't. They were too far away and after the heater on her car made the windows steam up, she'd had to roll a window down so cold air now poured through it. She shivered.

Lights. Hers were in a box in the attic. She hadn't put out any decorations. Not one. She just couldn't find her Christmas spirit.

I'll be Home for Christmas came on the radio. Again.

How many times is that now? Five? Six? Frank, I'm really tired of hearing you sing that song.

She changed the channel. This year the lights and music failed to move her, instead making her sad as she replayed memories of Christmas past with her family in her head. She'd be home for Christmas all right, but this time she'd be alone.

Jenna was as stuck in her sadness as if she'd found her feet frozen in an ice block. Stuck with no idea of how to move or how to thaw it.

Now she'd be spending the weekend with complete strangers while everyone back home got their holiday cheer on. It wasn't as if she had much of a social life these days. So it had been easy to say yes when the event organizer contacted her, looking for a replacement for an author who'd backed out. Jingle Bells came on the radio.

"Yeah, yeah, yeah. Dashing through the snow, jingle bells and ho, ho, ho."

Great. Now she was talking to herself. She really did need to get out among people.

Dark clouds moved in with the hint of bad weather as the sun disappeared behind the mountains like a curtain dropped upon the earth's stage, the dark clouds adding to her sadness. Driving during the night through mountains she'd never before visited delayed Jenna's arrival at the hotel.

Chyna, Jenna's former writing critique partner called Jenna's cell phone just as she pulled into the parking lot. "So how was the drive? You make it there okay?"

"I just pulled in. Can't talk now. I need to go in and register."

"You should've been there two hours ago."

"Yes, I know. Weather was bad. I'll call you later."

"All right. Have you seen Nicolo yet?"

"No. I'm still in my car. How could I have seen him already?"

Chyna could be so silly. She'd shown little interest in the event Jenna was attending until two days ago when she saw the flier and realized Nicolo Maldini, the handsome cover model and actor, would also attend. Chyna, who loved entertainment magazines and everything Hollywood, wanted the entire scoop on him.

"Well, get in there woman! What are you waiting for?"

Jenna rolled her eyes.

Waiting for you to get off the phone.

She'd never have actually said that to Chyna. Her former critique partner was the one person who always called to check on her. It was good to have someone who cared if she arrived safe after long hours on the road.

"I'll call you later."

"Okay. Keep your camera handy. Be sure to get pictures when you see him."

"I'll try."

"Don't mess up now. Don't just try. I'm expecting pics."

"Chyna, I'm really tired. I need to go."

"Later lady."

"Bye." She turned off the phone, dropped it into her purse and headed inside.

Inside the lobby, Christmas trees and garland greeted her while soft music played. The moment she walked in, the cheerful woman at the front desk whose nametag said Molly, greeted her. "Good evening."

"Good evening, Molly. I have a room for two nights. Jenna Heart."

"Oh yes. You're one of the authors. So glad you made it in safe before the weather changes. There's a snowstorm that's on its way. You came all the way from Memphis? That's quite a drive."

"It took me nearly eight hours."

Eight hours and six repetitions of I'll be Home for Christmas.

"Well, you can relax now. One key or two?"

"One. I still need to get dinner, but it doesn't look like there's much around here."

"You'd better hurry. The country restaurant next door, just up the hill, closes in less than an hour. There won't be anything else open this late around here."

"Thank you, Molly, I will." Jenna hurried to her room, freshened up and then walked to the restaurant. The temperature had dropped and the wind was picking up. She wrapped her scarf tighter around her neck against the wind as she climbed the steps to the restaurant. Inside, she stomped her feet and loosened her scarf.

The greeter sighed as Jenna approached.

Of course they want to close and go home soon, especially if bad weather is coming.

The greeter, whose nametag said Greta, answered the phone and eyed Jenna who stood waiting. She hung up and asked, "One?"

"Yes, just one. I haven't had dinner yet. Drove all the way from Memphis."

The woman grunted. "This way."

Jenna followed her to a small table near the kitchen door. Pots and pans rattled behind it.

There are plenty of other empty tables. Why seat me here? Because it's faster to clean up? Or because she just doesn't care? If I sit here, I'll have to listen to the kitchen noise.

She looked about the room. There were only eight other people in the restaurant. Two couples and a family of four who were leaving. Greta had such a sour expression and Jenna was tired. It was easier to sit and accept the menu than to ask to be moved. "Thank you, Greta."

The woman nodded and moved away.

Jenna glanced at the menu. Pots banged in the kitchen.

So noisy. I'll eat fast and go. The fastest thing to order would be a grilled cheese sandwich and a bowl of vegetable soup.

A young waitress with long red hair came over to the table. "Good evening. My name is Penny and I'll be your server. What would you like to drink?"

"Just water and I'll go ahead and order." She looked at her watch. "I know you close in thirty minutes, but I haven't had dinner. I just drove all the way from Memphis."

"That's a long way." Penny smiled. "I'll bet you're famished. What can I get you?"

"If you still have vegetable soup, I'd like a bowl of that and a grilled cheese sandwich."

"That's all? Yes, we have the soup. It'll be right up."

"Thank you, Penny."

"You're welcome."

Jenna sat back in her chair and relaxed, feeling less like she had to apologize for putting them out with her late night dinner request and relieved she'd made it before they closed. She watched as the other customers left, grateful she would be able to have a hot dinner.

The hotel and restaurant seemed empty yet there were plenty of cars parked at the hotel. Most writer events she'd attended in the past were full and authors would hang out in the lobby.

Wonder where the other attending authors are? Nicolo Maldini is supposed to be here for the book signing. Is he here already? Maybe there's a gathering I don't know about. Everyone must be here by now. Classes start tomorrow morning. It feels like I'm out of the loop. I've been away too long. But I had to be there for mother.

Penny brought Jenna's meal out right away. "Is there anything else I can get you?"

"No, this is fine. Thank you."

"All right. Well, let me know if you need anything."

"Yes, I will."

Jenna took a bite of soup, which was warm and delicious, but good as it was, she missed having someone to share meals with.

Santa, if there's one thing I want for Christmas more than anything, it's someone to spend Christmas with, not as an afterthought invitation because they feel sorry for me, but someone who really wants me to be there.

She was tired of feeling lonely and sad and it was harder because of the holidays.

After Jenna finished eating, she walked back to the hotel, unloaded her car and carried everything up to her room. Books to sell, bookmarks, handouts for her talk and her special throat tea. After unpacking and preparing for the morning class she would teach, she ran a hot bubble bath to relax and help her sleep.

Just before bed, she gave thanks for her safe journey through the mountains and for her guardian angel. Every night before bed Jenna went through the list of things she was thankful for. When she lay back on her pillow, she fell into a peaceful sleep for the first time in nearly a year.

* * * *

Jenna woke before her alarm, rested and excited to be starting the conference. She hurried to get ready and then headed downstairs for the continental breakfast. The room was full of authors eating and chatting. After fixing a plate, she found an empty seat beside a man and a woman. "May I join you?"

"Of course." the woman smiled. "Please do. I'm Amy and this is my husband Brett."

"It's nice to meet you. I'm Jenna Heart."

"Nice to meet you, Jenna. This will get easier once we've all registered and have name tags."

"I'm glad. I don't know a soul here and I just got in from Memphis last night."

"Well, you do now," Amy said. "We drove up from Florida."

"Oh, that's a drive!"

"Yes. I'm with Loving Hearts magazine and we're one of the sponsors of this event. Did you hear that Nicolo Maldini and his mother are joining us for dinner tonight?"

"No, I didn't. How sweet of him to bring his mother."

"Yes, it is. She's a breast cancer survivor and they're very close."

"Oh, I didn't know that. It's scary when you think you might lose them." Jenna paused, remembering. "I think it's great he's bringing her. He sounds like a nice guy."

"He is. And so good looking. He's also single." Amy winked. "Have you been to his website and fan page?"

"No, I've only seen his picture on the promotional materials for this weekend."

I can't let on when I meet him that I haven't seen his pictures and don't know much about him. Cover models can be so focused on themselves and he might be insulted. I should've looked him up online. But I had to scramble to get copies of my books in and bookmarks. Things I would've had in stock if I hadn't taken so much time away.

"Most women would have been at least a little bit curious." Amy gave her a measuring look. "I think you might be the only woman here who hasn't been to his site at least once."

"Well, I…" Jenna took a deep breath and then exhaled. "I've been taking care of my mother who was very ill. I just haven't had time."

She hadn't planned to say anything. Had planned not to in fact. She wanted the people she met this weekend to get to know her as Jenna Heart the author not Jenna the caretaker. That role was done. She didn't want people feeling sorry for her.

"Well, then of course you haven't had time to play on the Internet." Amy's expression was understanding and kind. "How is your mother now?"

"She passed a few months ago after a lengthy illness."

Amy's hand closed over hers. "Oh Jenna. I'm so sorry to hear that. You have my deepest sympathies."

"Thank you. I'm back to writing and able to attend author events again. I've been away too long. It's been a hurried scramble to get everything together in time."

Any gave her hand a slight squeeze and then released it. "Well I'm glad you're back."

Jenna smiled. "Me too."

Soon everyone had registered and the classes began. When it was Jenna's turn to teach, everything came back to her like slipping into a warm slipper. The class exercise was one of her favorites to teach because her students liked it so much. She began to relax and look forward to the rest of the weekend. She'd look up Nicolo's website before they went to dinner if there was time.

After classes ended everyone disbursed to their rooms to get ready for dinner. As Jenna fussed over her makeup, her hand shook slightly and she had to clean up mascara goofs. It took her longer than usual. It had been so long. Who bothered with makeup when tending to a dying parent? Her mascara would have run more than stayed had she worn it. Tonight, everyone would be dressed for dinner and she needed to look nice.

Knowing it would be cold on Bays Mountain tonight and they'd be outside listening to the wolves, she'd planned to wear black pants, black boots, a warm long sleeved top, a lighter weight jacket to match and had a long lined raincoat with a hood to wear over it. Scarf and gloves completed the outfit. Everything went together in earth tones and black, a classic look, but now as she looked into the mirror she looked somber. Not festive. She hadn't been thinking festive when she packed. She'd been thinking warm.

Well, I'm the woman writing the romances, the woman behind the books, not the woman on the cover. It's not like I need to look like the beautiful women on my covers. I'll just be that woman in the background as usual.

Though she did hunt in her bag for the tube of red lipstick, before wiping off the rosy color she'd been wearing and applying a festive red color to her lips.

The moment she stepped off the elevator downstairs and saw Nicolo Maldini standing on the other side of the room she wished she'd worn something prettier. Something sexier, like that woman next to him in the red dress with the long blonde hair.

I should've looked him up online, even if it made me late.

She took a few steps away from the elevator and stood near the hallway taking him in. Tall, well built, dark and incredibly handsome with dark brown eyes and a wonderful smile. There was something in the air about him and it wasn't twinkling Christmas lights. No, it was as if he put out his own light, the kind of man who could light up a room the moment he entered.

Nicolo Maldini stood with his mother, Angela Maldini, a petite blonde haired woman who didn't look her age. They stood beside the Christmas tree near the door. He was handsome in the good looking all American kind of way. Women clustered around him wanting pictures. He was including his mother in each picture.

How sweet. It says a lot about the kind of son he is. Good to his mama.

Jenna smiled at the sweetness of the scene. Seeing them standing with the bright colored tree and lights behind them warmed her heart where the sadness over missing her mother lingered. The warmth between mother and son was beautiful to see.

Hovering back near the hallway where she could watch but not be noticeable, Jenna felt less like going up to say hello as old insecurities kicked in the way they always did around handsome men. Naturally shy, keeping to herself came easy to her and she felt herself falling into that old pattern.

Nicolo was a son who clearly adored his mother. He could've been caught up in ego, eating up all the attention while his mother stood at the sidelines, but he wasn't. Instead she stood by his side and he stood with his arm around her, including her in everything. It was nice to see. From what Jenna had seen so far, she could really like Nicolo Maldini.

He seemed so nice. Considerate and thoughtful.

And he was handsome, so handsome she couldn't stop looking at him. There was something about his deep brown eyes that pulled her to him.

No, I am not going all fan girl. I know better.

Amy came over to her. "Aren't you going to go up and have your picture taken with Nicolo?"

"I know I ought to get a photo with him like everyone else but I just can't."

"You're shy." Amy smiled.

"A little." Jenna nodded. "I just don't do the fan girl thing. It's just not me."

Once was enough.

Rick, the captain of the football team in her freshman year of high school thought he was Gods gift to women. He'd dated her but when after six months she'd still not slept with him, holding out until she was engaged, he hadn't dumped her. Instead he'd let her catch him with Missy Sue, who'd been on her knees in the locker room. "This is how you do it," he'd said. "Worship the cock, baby. Show her how it's done." Missy Sue smirked and continued on and Jenna who'd never seen an erection before was shocked into tears before she turned and ran.

Thinking back on it now, Jenna wondered how she'd fallen for such a jerk. He had nothing to offer beyond his good looks. What a thing to say to a young teenage girl. She couldn't have thought that one up for her books. Her mind didn't work that way and if she hadn't heard him say it with her own ears she'd never have believed someone would talk that way.

After that event, men who were well built and handsome didn't make her all aflutter the way they did other women. She wasn't getting on her knees and worshipping anyone or anything.

Though she did want to meet Nicolo. Something in the depths of his eyes called to something deep within her.

That longing must have shown in her face because Amy said, "Come on, I'll go up with you."

"All right."

She had to get over this thing from the past. This wasn't high school.

Amy kept her talking until they were in front of Nicolo and then he was looking at Jenna with those deep brown eyes which made her want to melt and she had to say something, anything before the silence stretched too long.

"Hello, Nicolo. I'm Jenna Heart."

He gave her a warm welcoming smile as his firm, warm hand reached for and now held hers. "Pleased to meet you Jenna Heart."

Everything about him spoke of warmth and heat. The kind of heat only an adult male, fit and in his prime, could exude.

"Nice to meet you." she replied, decidedly warm and wondering if her face was bright pink.

"This is my mother, Angela."

"Pleased to meet you." She gave his mother a smile and then heard Nicolo speak and turned her attention back to him.

"Are you going to dinner with us?" His gaze focused entirely on her made her feel giddy and shy all at once.

"Yes, I'm looking forward to it."

Two other women pressed forward and Jenna moved back before he could say anything more. It all happened so fast. There was no time for a photo with him now. Everyone was pairing up to carpool to the Bays Mountain Park and Planetarium where they'd hear a program about the wolves while they ate dinner.

She rode up to Bays Mountain with another author named Dora. They found their way by following the car in front of them through a light drizzle of rain up to a large log building in a heavily wooded area. Gray and drizzly, the area was dark and calm. Not one sound gave away the location of the wolves though they had to be near.

Once inside, everyone seemed to have already made plans to sit together in groups as they went to the tables and filled them.

Many of these women already know each other. Amy and Brett's table is full.

Jenna took a seat on the other side of the room. Too far to see Nicolo. She learned her tablemates weren't with the author reader weekend and had only come to hear the talk on the wolves. Jenna felt isolated, though the people at her table were nice enough. They only wanted to talk about wolves, which Jenna knew little about.

Dinner was delicious and the wolf specialist and park naturalist spoke about the wolves on the mountain. Wolves could be solitary creatures but they mated for life. Fascinated, she listened and ate. Desert was sweeter than she was used to, her head buzzed from the sugar.

After dinner, the park naturalist invited everyone to walk over to edge of the wolf sanctuary to hear the wolves. Though he warned the rain might make them quieter than usual.

She followed the group down the path until they all stood waiting and listening. Drizzling rain colored everything silver dark and shiny as it came down. The cold began to chill her along with the drizzle, which had dampened her scarf, and everything it touched beyond her raincoat.

One lone wolf howled. The sound, one of the most lonesome and eerie things she'd ever heard.

Another wolf joined in, the sounds sending a cold chill into her bones. She shivered. Goose bumps covered her skin. Rain was running down her face past her hood and she could hardly see. She had the primitive urge to run brought on by the sound of wolves howling in the dark night. She shivered again, wrapping her arms closer about herself.

The rain stopped running down her face and nose as an umbrella appeared over her head. She turned to look up.

Nicolo.

CHAPTER TWO

Nicolo towered over Jenna, protecting her from the rain, holding an umbrella.

The shivery frightened feeling brought on by the wolves howls and the dark, rainy woods dissipated along with her goose bumps beneath the warmth of his eyes and the protection he offered. He was tall, strong, solid and unafraid. She smiled up at him. "Thank you."

"You looked cold."

"I am." The wolves howled again and she jumped.

"They won't hurt you."

"I know. I just… well, the sounds they make. It's so…" She trailed off feeling foolish, but unable to stop herself she glanced in the direction where the howls had come from. She frowned. "It's not a sound you want to hear in the dark of night. Even though I know they're in an enclosure, there's something primitive and frightening about it."

"Fight or flight response."

"Flight." She looked up at him, her eyes wide, and her breath short. "For me, it's flight."

He smiled. "You're safe Jenna." His voice was calm and

unworried, his breathing slow and steady. He paused, smiling at her and then his eyes crinkled further as his smile deepened. "Don't run."

We're only talking about wolves. Weren't we? No. His tone and his eyes were saying something more. Teasing or testing.

The others had moved further down the path to get closer to the wolves even though it was unlikely they'd see them in the dark rainy woods.

"So, Jenna Heart. Is that your real name? Or a pseudonym?"

"It's my real name." She noticed then that Nicolo's mother stood nearby holding her own large umbrella.

His mother moved closer. "That's a good name for a romance writer."

"Yes, I've been blessed. Mother wanted to name me Hannah. But my dad said no, that was too many H's."

Nicolo and his mother both smiled. "I think you father was right," Angela said.

"Smart man," Nicolo said.

"Yes he was," Jenna smiled. "I wish he'd lived long enough to know I was writing books. I wish he'd been able to hold my first book in his hands and seen Jenna Heart right there on the cover."

"My mom raised me and my sister by herself," Nicolo said. "She was a single mom."

"That had to be hard. I was in high school when we lost my dad in a car accident. Then it was just mother and me."

"No siblings?"

Jenna shook her head.

The group had returned. "Time to head back," the park naturalist said. "We'll be closing up once you folks leave."

Everyone filed back up the path, Nicolo still holding the umbrella over Jenna's head. His phone went off and he took it out of his pocket, looked at it, frowned and answered. "Hello." He listened and then said, "There's nothing more to say. Stop calling me. I told you I'd be out of town." He hung up and put the phone away.

Back at the lodge, everyone was now saying goodnight and heading to their cars. Jenna had been waiting on Nicolo to finish his call so she could thank him. "Good night," Jenna said. "Thank you for letting me stand under your umbrella."

"You're welcome, any time." He nodded, seeming pre-occupied now. "See you tomorrow."

Jenna walked to meet Dora over by her van. "Wow," Dora said. "Sharing an umbrella with Nicolo. Lucky girl. I'll bet that was fun."

Fun? Well, she wouldn't have called it fun. Though she'd enjoyed every minute. She'd been too unnerved by the wolves to be in a fun frame of mind. The way he'd eased her mind helped.

"It was really nice," she said. "He's so gentlemanly."

"I'll bet. He's a dream." Dora turned the windshield wipers on a faster mode. "What did he say?"

"We talked about the wolves mostly."

"Mostly. Mmm hmm." Dora cranked the heat up in the van. "Not sure I'd care what we talked about if he turned those melt making eyes on me."

"Melt making?"

"You know. The kind where they look at you and everything wants to melt and go all liquid like molten lava."

"Oh yes, those kind of eyes." Jenna nodded. "He does have those."

The way he'd looked at her tonight, she'd dreamed of deep brown eyes looking at her like that. Dreams like those she put into her romance novels. She hadn't written in a long while. Everything in her normal life had been put on hold. But she now had the feeling this weekend was going to change all that.

Once back at the hotel the chilling rain was coming down even harder. Jenna and Dora ran from the van to the entrance and shook off the raindrops then headed to their rooms.

Jenna took a hot shower to warm up and then put on flannel pajamas and made a cup of hot cocoa. A rare treat, one of her comforting things. She slipped under the covers, propped up the pillows and dialed Chyna.

Waiting for her to answer, she sipped the cocoa, remembering back when she was younger and had sleepovers during Christmas break. All the girls would sit or lounge around in their pajamas with their cocoa and cookies. Homemade cookies her mother always made. Gingerbread men and star sugar cookies. That had been years ago and it had been years since she'd thought about it.

Chyna answered on the fourth ring. "Girlfriend! Tell me you finally got to meet Nicolo."

Well, hello to you too. Jenna suppressed a grin. *Chyna was so predictable.*

"I did meet him."

"Ooh! Details, I want details."

"Well I met him and his mother briefly before we left for the dinner at the wolf sanctuary, but I couldn't get any pictures."

"Sneak them if he's not posing for any. Take them fast before he notices."

"Oh, I think he'd notice. He seems like a man who notices things."

"Well, do it anyway. Don't go all shy like you usually do. No wonder you don't have any boyfriends. You have to actually talk to men, Jenna. They aren't going to come chasing after you."

"He's posing for them. There just wasn't time to get one with him before we had to leave for dinner."

"Oh. Well get one tomorrow. Get plenty. Seriously now, you've got to take pics so you can post them on your website for your readers."

"Okay, I will tomorrow."

"So, what was he wearing? How did he look? What did he say?"

"Well, he's here with his mother, Angela and introduced me to her. They both seemed real nice."

"Girlfriend, you think everyone is nice. But go on, what was he wearing?"

"Dark slacks and a nice shirt. Dressy, but not too dressy. His mama looked real pretty and I'd never have guessed she was old enough to be his mother."

"I don't care about his mother. What did he say? Was he as hot in person?"

"He's tall, at least six foot and he has the most amazing eyes."

Chyna sighed. "Dreamy. You are so lucky."

"It was a real nice evening." Jenna sipped her cocoa.

"You're back early though. It's only ten thirty. And on a Friday night, too. But maybe he's not partying since he has his mother with him. That has to be a drag, taking his mother everywhere with him."

"I don't think he sees it that way. He seemed happy to have her with him. I think he enjoys her company."

Chyna snorted. "He's an actor. And he's a red blooded Italian American male. You can't tell me he wouldn't rather be out getting some."

"Chyna. You don't even know the man."

"Like you do?"

"Well what I know is that he is thoughtful and considerate. When we were outside listening to the wolves, he came up behind me and shared his umbrella and even asked me if I was cold."

"Ooh! He did? Honey, that was your moment. What did you say?"

"I just said yes, I was cold and I thanked him for sharing his umbrella."

Chyna groaned. "Of course you did. When you could have said something like, you can warm me up any time, or not now that you're here or I might be cold outside but I'm hot inside."

"Chyna. I can't say something like that to a man I just met. That's just not me."

"And there's the problem. Look, you've got to be more assertive and stop holding back with men. A hot man like that doesn't want some shy little mouse. He wants a sexy, assertive woman. And you've got to stand out to get his attention. He's shared his umbrella to be nice, sure, but now he's forgotten all about you. He probably doesn't even remember your name or what you look like."

Jenna went quiet and still.

Why did I call her again?

The call had turned into another pick on Jenna session, which was not what she needed right now.

"Okay, well, I'm really tired now. I need to go."

"All right. Get your beauty rest girlfriend. And give me a call tomorrow."

"Okay. Night."

"Goodnight."

Jenna hung up the phone and sat looking into her cup of half drunk cocoa which had gone cool. Kind of like their friendship. It had its warm moments but often she was left feeling disappointed in her friend.

The days of flannel pajamas, cocoa, cookies and giggles with a close girlfriend into the night are long gone. Everything changes once girls start chasing boys. I don't know why I even thought of that tonight.

She placed the cup on the nightstand and turned off the light.

Fixing the pillows, she lay down on her side and curled up.

He's forgotten all about me. Of course he has. Chyna is right. Why would he remember a quiet mouse like me? Whereas I'll remember the way he looked at me for the rest of my life.

Jenna sighed and tried her best to fall asleep. After a while she realized she hadn't gone through her list of thankful things for the day. No wonder she couldn't sleep. She closed her eyes and counted off.

One, Amy and Brett were nice and I'm glad I met them. Two, my class went well. Three, dinner was good. Four, I met Nicolo Maldini. Five, Nicolo shared his umbrella with me.

It was funny how once she got through her list, she felt better and sleepier. Her thoughts were happier and more restful. She went right to sleep.

Halfway though the night, a strange dream woke her. She got up to go to the bathroom and her head swam. Pounding now, she wondered if she'd be sick, if she'd caught something or if it was a migraine coming on. Something she hadn't had in a long time. Whatever the dream had been that woke her, it was gone now.

By four a.m. she knew she had a migraine. An incredibly strong one. She'd never be able to teach her class if it kept up. Usually once one came on this strong, it did not go away with meds and they only way to get rid of it was to sleep it off. She went back to bed hoping it would be gone when she woke.

Sleep eluded her and throbbing was her constant companion. Finally, when she thought someone might be opening the rooms for the events, she threw on her clothes and moved slowly downstairs. She had to tell them she wouldn't be able to teach and to hand off the handouts so they'd at least have something for showing up. She felt terrible about letting everyone down, but she couldn't help it.

Downstairs she met one of the sponsors, whose name escaped her at the moment as she could hardly think.

The woman said, "I'll tell everyone and see the materials are handed out. Everyone will understand. Now you just go back to bed and get well."

Jenna went to her room, took as many pain relievers as she felt her body could handle and went back to bed.

She slept five hours and woke with only a slight remnant of the headache. Moving slowly she showered and prepared for the book signing.

When she went downstairs to meet everyone in the lobby, Amy came over to her. "Are you feeling better?"

"Yes, it's just a slight headache now. A low throb."

"Are you sure you're up for the book signing?"

"Yes, I'll be all right. I've been sleeping. Took more pain meds when I got up and I'm bringing water to drink." Jenna fished in her purse for her car keys.

They walked outside to get ready to carpool again. Jenna held her keys in one hand and her bottle of water in the other. Her car was just a few feet away and she clicked her key fob to unlock it.

"Were you planning to drive?" Amy asked.

"Yes."

Brett had pulled their car in front of the hotel. "Our car is right here and we have room for one more," Amy said. "Why don't you ride with us? You're just barely over that migraine."

"Oh. Well, all my books and things are in my trunk."

Nicolo and Brett approached them and had overheard. "Where are they?" Brett asked. "We'll get them."

"Thank you." She turned to Amy. "Yes. I'd like to ride with you. Thank you. This is so thoughtful of you."

"We're happy to have you ride with us," Amy said.

Brett popped his trunk and he and Nicolo followed her over to her car where she popped her trunk and showed them the two boxes she needed.

"That's not much," Brett said. "Is that everything?"

"Yes. It's just my books and my bookmarks."

The men had the boxes stowed in Brett's trunk and had it closed up before she realized Nicolo would be riding with them.

Oh my. Wait until Chyna hears about this. I'll be riding to and from the signing with Nicolo.

Amy got into the car in back with Jenna and Nicolo rode up front with Brett. Jenna sank into the soft leather seats and rested with a silent sigh.

Amy is right. This is much more restful. I've never been to the town and know nothing about the bookstore. Now I can rest and not worry about getting there on time. All I have to do is arrive and set up my books at my table.

"Thank you, Amy. This is much more restful than trying to find the bookstore and driving while following the map."

Amy smiled at her. "You just rest and enjoy the ride."

Throughout this exchange Jenna had felt Nicolo listening as he sat deleting messages out of his phone. He seemed to have many, but that must be the life of an actor. He put away his phone and then turned to her. "Are you feeling better?"

"Yes, I am now that I've rested. I'm not sure what brought on that terrible headache but I'm thinking maybe too much sugar. I don't eat processed sugar at home, only honey. The dessert last night may have caused it. I knew after we finished dinner that I'd had too much sugar and then I went ahead and had hot cocoa before I went to bed."

Amy, who was an herbalist, joined the conversation and the three of them talked about healthy eating practices, a conversation Jenna enjoyed. None of her friends ate healthy. She'd started making changes after her mother became ill. Jenna was determined to live a long and healthy life, though friends like Chyna urged her to eat sweets and salty foods. It had taken over a month to break her sugar addiction and now she couldn't eat much of it.

Nicolo went to the gym twice a day and was enthusiastic about the subject of fitness.

It's so nice to be able to converse with him about healthy eating choices and have him not only get it, but be far ahead of me with it. Instead of being made to feel like a weirdo or a freak, he makes me feel normal. Like I'm making good choices. Which I know I am.

And every time he turned in his seat to look at her, his eyes lit upon her with a light that made happiness well up inside her. The stress and tension of the headache was long gone. She really was enjoying this ride.

He's nowhere near like the guys Chyna tries to fix me up with. I can be myself and he's accepting me the way I am. He's so nice. He can't be how Chyna keeps saying he is. He's natural and down to earth. The kind of person you meet and feel like you've known all your life, because of the ease of the conversation. Now I wish I'd gone online earlier to look at his website. I want to know more about him. Tonight for sure I will look. Tonight.

When they reached the bookstore, Brett parked in the lot across the street and they got out and unloaded the boxes. Brett and Amy had boxes full from the magazine she worked for. Between the four of them everything got carried in with one trip.

Inside, the bookstore owner greeted them and then showed them to their tables. Jenna's table had her name on it, there was one author named Kara James next to her and then Nicolo.

Oh good.

Nicolo's table was set up with stacks of magazines. The cover featured two shots of Nicolo. One with his shirt off, wearing jeans and an intense look in his eyes, his gaze looking directly at her. In the other he was pulling his shirt off and looking away from the camera with a sexy smile.

Kara James had several erotic romances out. She introduced herself to Jenna and then said, "How steamy are your books? Have you tried writing erotica?"

"Well, I..." Jenna straightened the bookmarks on her table that hadn't moved from where she'd placed them. "No, mine aren't that steamy." She took a breath. "Mine aren't erotic romance. I'm not so good at writing those steamier sex scenes. Haven't had enough experience to draw from so I can't keep up with you all. But the one I'm writing now goes a little farther and is all about touch and tenderness. Because the heroine is craving that."

She glanced at Kara and saw Nicolo watching her before he looked away. He'd been listening. She blushed and stopped talking. She hadn't meant for him to overhear.

Customers started coming into the store. Everyone got busy signing and talking about their books. Ladies were drawn to Nicolo's table where he was signing magazine covers.

After a couple of hours there was a lull and Nicolo started signing magazines for the authors. He glanced over at Jenna. She'd been sitting and watching him, wishing he'd sign one for her. Reading her expression he said, "Would you like one?"

She smiled and said, "Yes, please."

Nicolo slid a magazine in front of him, picked up the pen and signed it for her. Then he reached behind Kara and handed the magazine to Jenna with a smile.

"Thank you," she smiled back at him as she took the magazine and then glanced down at it. Her eyes widened as she read what he'd written.

Jenna,

Hugs and kisses, Nicolo Maldini

There was an X and an O beside his name.

That wasn't what he'd written on any of the other magazines she'd seen him sign.

Oh my. Mine is unique.

She pulled the magazine close, treasuring it and keeping the words to herself, not wanting anyone to see them. Then she placed the magazine in her box, out of sight.

He'd gone on to sign a few more after signing hers, but now she became aware he was watching her stow it away like a treasure. She blushed.

When the signing was over, everyone boxed up what they had left and loaded the cars. Nicolo and Jenna were putting boxes in the trunk when she brushed against a paper that fell out of a box and sliced a paper cut against the side of her hand.

"Oh!" She pulled her hand close, grasping it with her other hand.

"What is it?" Nicolo said. "Paper cut? Let me see."

She held out her hand palm down, the side of her hand angled up so he could see it.

His warm, gentle fingers caressed her palm. "Those really sting."

"Yes, they do." She blinked away the watering in her eyes.

His fingertips caressed her palm while the warm strength of his hand made her feel comforted and cared for.

"I noticed you aren't wearing a ring."

The abrupt change of subject took her off guard.

A ring?

She looked down at her hands, her short, plain unpolished fingernails and wished now that she'd had a manicure. "Oh. No, I've never been married or engaged."

"You have beautiful hands."

She looked up at him. "Thank you."

He stroked her palm with a light touch. Tingles spread up her arm, every nerve ending coming alive.

"I haven't had time to get my nails done." She was out of the habit.

"Your nails are fine." Another light stroke from his fingertips pulled her attention away from her nails and back to the feelings his touch was invoking in her. "You look wonderful," he said.

The way he was looking at her made her feel beautiful. The tone of his voice along with his words made her feel lighter, giddy almost. Blushing from the attention along with the heat building in her body, she looked down again, shy.

He raised her hand and kissed it, his lips warm upon her skin. "All better?"

"Yes, better." Her voice came out breathy like an old time movie star. Sounds she'd never made before.

Nicolo smiled. "Good."

Amy and Brett were approaching. Nicolo released her hand. "You'll be at dinner?"

"Yes."

"Good." He smiled.

On the way back to the hotel they discussed the success of the signing and the upcoming holidays. Throughout the ride, Jenna remembered the feel of his touch and his kiss upon her skin.

When they got back to the hotel, there was a floral delivery for Nicolo waiting. More than a dozen red roses with greenery.

He picked up the card, read it and then stuck it in his pocket before picking them up to carry to his room. He seemed a bit preoccupied. "See you tonight," he said with a nod.

"Yes, see you tonight," Jenna said.

"Ring me when you're ready," Amy said.

He nodded and moved on down the hall.

"I wonder if the ladies send him flowers," Amy said.

"He must have a girlfriend." Jenna said, as her heart dropped. Maybe he flirted with all the ladies as he had with her. Maybe he didn't find her special in any way.

"Oh, I don't know. You'll have to ask him that tonight."

Jenna's eyes widened. "I couldn't ask him that."

"Fine, then I will." Amy winked.

* * * *

Getting ready for the Christmas party Jenna donned a soft red sweater, black skirt, hose and heels. Tonight she'd be festive. The Christmas party for the authors and organizers was at the organizers private home instead of the hotel. Jenna gave a ride to Ann who'd flown in and didn't have a car.

"Welcome," Gloria, the event organizer, opened the door and

greeted Jenna and Ann with a smile. "Come in and let me take your coats."

Gloria's home was welcoming and all decked out with Christmas trees, lights and presents. Gloria was as welcoming as her home. Nicolo and his mother were already inside chatting with the guests. Nicolo was wearing a red shirt and black pants that set off his dark coloring. His dark eyes lit up when he saw Jenna.

"How'd you like to unwrap him Christmas morning?" Jenna overheard one of the authors say under her breath.

The thought of unwrapping Nicolo, unbuttoning his shirt button by button down to his pants made Jenna's face heat until she was sure she was as red as her sweater. Santa Baby played and Nicolo watched her with a slight smile. That was the sexiest Christmas song she'd ever heard and he was the sexiest man she'd ever seen. She felt her face getting hotter.

He has to know the effect he has on women. Did he hear what that woman said? Even if he didn't, my face always shows everything.

Jenna wanted to hide under the dining room table until her thoughts and face cooled down. People began to move through the kitchen filling their plates. "Come on," Amy said. She picked up a plate and handed it to Jenna. "Everything looks delicious."

It was quite a spread. Good home cooked food and plenty of it. Jenna walked through with Amy, commenting on the food and then paused at the dining room entrance. Nicolo and his mother were just sitting down at the table.

"Come and join us," Angela said.

He looked at his phone, frowned and answered it. "Hello. Yes I got them. Thank you. But you have to stop this. Save your money. Now I have to go."

Somehow Jenna ended up sitting in between Nicolo and his

mother. Both seemed happy to be dining with her. They made her feel so welcome she lost her shyness.

He's not the sort of actor Chyna described at all. He's so nice.

The topic turned to exercise. Weightlifting ran in the Maldini family. Even Nicolo's mother worked out.

"You work out with your mom?"

"Yes, we do. Mom and me, we both enjoy a good workout."

"You must also enjoy each other's company."

"We do," he said.

"Oh yes, we do," Angela chimed in and they shared loving glances and smiles.

Chyna was so wrong about Nicolo. He wanted his mother to be here this weekend, enjoyed her company and didn't feel she was a burden at all.

"I used to work out at the gym three times a week. I did yoga and aqua zumba. But I wasn't able to renew my rec center membership this year or to work out much because I was taking care of my mom."

Angela's face showed concern. "Your mother was ill?"

"Yes, she had cancer. She passed after being on hospice. I'm glad I was able to be with her, even though I had to give up a lot of things to do it."

"I'm sorry for your loss," Nicolo said.

"Thank you."

Angela touched Jenna's arm. "I've worked at hospice so I know how it is. It's a blessing to spend those last days with them but so hard to lose them. I'll pray for you."

Tears welled up in Jenna's eyes. "Thank you."

They were both so kind and caring. Genuinely caring.

Jenna didn't know why she'd once again told people she'd just met about her mother when she'd planned not to. But she was glad she had. If Angela worked hospice, then she understood. It was the sort of thing no one really knew unless they'd experienced it themselves. Not everyone could spend every day with the dying.

"The hospice workers were like angels. Hospice was so good to us both. The work you do is a blessing."

Another author ducked into the room. "The cakes and pies have been cut if anyone wants dessert."

"Oh, I don't know." Jenna looked at her plate. "I'm so full already. And I need to lose a few pounds." She looked at Nicolo. "I need to get back to working out. You must work out pretty heavy and intense to look the way you do."

"I break it up. Do my cardio and abs in the morning on an empty stomach and do weight training in the afternoon."

"Wow that's a busy day. I really need to start doing something. It's hard when I travel to events to get exercise in."

"I'm working out in the hotel gym tomorrow morning if you want to join me. It's early though. Six a.m."

"Yes, I'd like that. I need the exercise and it's hard to get it in when I travel."

"Great. Then come work out with me."

"I might."

They stood and took their plates to the kitchen. Jenna eyed the desserts but after the migraine, which could have been caused by too much sugar the other night, she decided to stay out of them. She headed into the living room to mingle with the other guests.

On her way back from the kitchen after refilling her glass, she passed Nicolo.

"So you're coming to workout with me tomorrow, right?"

"Yes."

"What's your room number?"

Jenna was floored.

He wants my room number?

CHAPTER THREE

Though Jenna had never done such a thing in her life, she gave Nicolo her room number. It flowed off of her tongue as naturally as if she did this sort of thing every day. But at the same time her mind raced.

What in the world am I doing? Even if he seems like a super nice guy and he's here with his mother and they've both been really nice and it's probably innocent, we're only going to work out after all. Still, what were you thinking?

And that was the thing. When he looked down into her eyes and asked the question, she wasn't thinking at all. Instead, she was caught up in feeling and her response was automatic.

A sense of panic came over her, triggering the need to run.

What have I done? I don't give my room number out to men, ever. I can't stay here. I have to go.

Nicolo had moved into the other room to chat with the ladies there.

I'll slip out and maybe he won't notice.

Ann, who'd ridden with her to the party needed to get back. She had a flight to catch. She'd been trying to catch Jenna's eye and hinting she was ready to go.

"Let's go." Jenna ducked into the kitchen, and threw away her cup and nodded to Ann. "I'm ready if you are."

They collected their coats and headed toward the door. Rounding the corner, Jenna realized Nicolo stood there and she'd have to walk past him.

"You're leaving already?" Nicolo gazed at her, surprised, his phone in his hand.

Yes. No. Yes.

Under his intent gaze she felt flustered, part of her wanting to say no, I'll stay. But the urge to run was too strong and even his gaze and his voice could hot hold her.

"I have to go." She spoke quick fighting the urge to run out the door. She had their hostess to thank and everyone to say goodbye to. It would've been rude to run out. But she hurried through the goodbyes nonetheless. She needed to go.

Ann seemed in a hurry too and helped with saying goodbye and getting out the door, as everyone knew she had a flight to catch. After the goodbyes they headed to Jenna's car. Halfway there, Ann said, "You don't have to hurry so fast. We have time."

"Okay." Jenna slowed her pace; glad Nicolo was in the house and wouldn't see her scurrying away to her car after the door closed. She'd surprised him by leaving so soon but he couldn't know the reason why. She wasn't sure herself.

Once in the car, Jenna realized the real reason she was running. She'd run from Nicolo and what might happen. Running because the way he looked at her made her want to say yes to everything. Something she'd never done before. And that simple fact scared her. He'd made her breathy and she could still feel the touch of his fingers upon her skin. The man exuded sexual charisma like a fountain and she felt drawn to him in such a strong way it was frightening to her.

She was not prepared for the intensity of Nicolo.

This wasn't one of the sweet slow romance stories she wrote about where the hero wooed the girl slow and with sweet kisses to bring her out of her shyness. This was a deep, wild desire, which lay within her. One that she'd never known existed. And he had awakened it. She was running from herself as much as from him. From the wild, deep part of her that had awakened.

On the way back to the hotel, Ann carried most of the conversation while Jenna tried to follow the GPS and take her mind off of Nicolo.

Why is it so hard to get back to the hotel? To simply go back the way we came? And why can't I concentrate on this, where my mind should be, instead of on Nicolo Maldini?

"Nicolo is a very handsome man." Jo Ann said.

"Yes. He is."

"He seemed to have his eyes on you tonight. He was showing you plenty of attention."

"Really? I don't know why he'd be interested in me. He meets so many beautiful cover models and actresses. I'm nowhere in that league. I'm just the girl who writes the romances, not the girl on the covers. And besides, some woman sent him roses. He probably has a girlfriend."

"Maybe you're not a cover model, but you do have that girl next door thing going for you. Some men really go for that. And those roses could be from anyone."

"I suppose." She frowned at the GPS. "I hope we're going the right way."

Ann turned her attention to reading road signs and Jenna was glad the subject had changed. She'd been called the girl next-door type before, but even so, Nicolo Maldini was way out of her league.

Though he did ask for my room number.

That simple fact remained, much as she tried to push the subject away.

They reached the hotel and as Jenna parked, Ann said, "Thank you for giving me a ride. I know it meant you had to leave the party earlier than you planned and it was sweet of you. I appreciate it."

"Oh, I didn't mind. I was happy to help and you're quite welcome." They got out and she shut and locked the doors. "Have a nice safe flight home and a Merry Christmas."

"You too. Merry Christmas and a safe drive home."

Back inside the hotel lobby, Jenna glanced around at the Christmas decorations again, thinking how cozy it was. Too bad she couldn't spend Christmas here. This had been a good weekend, getting her out and away from her computer, back among friendly people. She sighed, resigned to spending Christmas home alone.

I'll be home for Christmas started playing in the lobby. Jenna sighed. It was an instrumental version, but she knew all the words and they would run through her head. This Christmas song seemed to be following her around this season, coming as a reminder. Like she needed one.

Seven times for this song. And who knows how many times I'll have to listen to it again before I get home?

She'd forgotten about being alone while she was at the party, enjoying Nicolo and Angela's company. She'd felt the first holiday cheer she'd had all season.

Now it was back to reality. Reality and a long drive home to a cold empty house. And here she was, back at the hotel already, while everyone else was still at the party. Everyone had been nice, but between shyness and sadness she'd held back like that girl at the edge of the dance who watches with longing but never gets up the courage to do more than watch.

This is no way to live my life. I need to stop that. It's time to start really living.

Getting ready for bed, she made a cup of hot cocoa. She looked at the magazine Nicolo had signed for her and touched it with her fingertips as a soft smile spread across her face.

Hugs and kisses. I like that. So sweet and romantic.

Still wearing a smile she carried her cup of cocoa over to the bedside table and set it down before climbing into bed. Pulling the covers up she reached for her cocoa and the paperback book she'd brought to read.

I am not calling Chyna. Tonight I want to remember all the little things Nicolo has said and done and I'm not sharing them with anyone. Tomorrow I'll talk to Chyna.

She closed her eyes and went through her thankful list.

One, that migraine went away so I could attend the book signing. Two, Amy and Brett invited me to ride with them and it was restful and fun. Three, Nicolo rode with us and I enjoyed talking to him Four, Nicolo signed my magazine in a special way that makes me happy. Five, Nicolo and Angela were so nice and dinner is a happy memory.

She paused. Should she go past five? She'd always stopped at five.

Nicolo asked me to come work out with him and his mom. He asked for my room number. Was it a good thing he asked? Should I be thankful?

Knowing she could toss this around in her head all evening, she picked up her book and read until she got sleepy.

* * * *

Jenna was up by six a.m. wondering if Nicolo was in the hotel exercise room. He hadn't called.

Why did he ask for my room number if he wasn't going to call? Men are so confusing. Maybe he's already down there. Maybe he forgot my room number.

She threw on her workout clothes and brushed her teeth, then washed her face and combed her hair. Then she headed down to the first floor where the exercise room was, her stomach doing little flips as she rode in the elevator.

Would he be there?

She wasn't used to working out on an empty stomach. Usually she had toast or something along with her tea. But she'd also never worked out at six a.m. She found the workout room and eased open the door. The room was empty.

He's not here. Guess I got up earlier than usual to work out by myself.

She walked over to the treadmill and climbed on and set a pace to warm up.

At least in here there's no Christmas music playing.

There was no music, just the sound of the treadmill. She was alone with her thoughts.

Now I can really tell it's been too long since I worked out. Everything is stiff. That long drive and then sitting in classes, not moving around as much as at home. That was one problem with writer's events, all the sitting and not enough exercise.

Walking felt good now. She'd warmed up and worked some of the morning kinks out. She upped the pace of the machine.

This feels great. But really, do I need a machine to get a walking workout?

She'd let lack of an exercise room stop her from working out when she traveled.

There's no reason I can't go for a walk no matter where I'm staying. Stepping outside for fresh air would be a good thing and no exercise room is needed for that.

She finished her workout, glad she'd done it and glad Nicolo had suggested it. She didn't need him to get a workout, though she might not have done it otherwise. She'd fallen into bad habits, taking care of everyone else but herself.

It's too bad he's not here so I could thank him.

She turned off the machine and stepped off. She drank half her water bottle and then headed for the breakfast room.

No sign of Nicolo or Angela. Maybe they've gone home already. Well at least he won't see me all sweaty and red faced.

She picked up a napkin and dabbed at her face.

Her appetite was back in a strong way and she felt great. She filled her plate, grabbed orange juice then sat. It wasn't so bad eating by herself this morning now that she was feeling good.

After breakfast, she went out to the front desk where she learned the snow, which had fallen all night and was still falling, had made the roads on her route home difficult. The front desk clerk, Molly asked if she wanted to extend her stay another night at the reduced rate.

"I'll get back with you on that," she said.

"That's fine. Just let us know."

She headed up to her room and turned on the TV to the weather channel, watching as they showed her route home would have plenty of snow and ice. She didn't mind traveling through snow, but ice she wanted to avoid.

The smart thing to do was stay put. The snowstorm would move through and she'd leave tomorrow. If nothing else, she'd stay in her room and write. There was no reason to hurry home. No one to be home for. She called the front desk and confirmed the room for another night.

After her shower she slipped on a robe and climbed onto the bed with her laptop to write.

Her phone rang.

Chyna. She's up early.

"Hey lady. Have you seen the weather forecast?"

"Yes I have and I've decided to stay another night."

"Then I won't worry. Did you get those pics of Nicolo?"

"I had one taken with him at the Christmas party last night."

"Just one? But he was around all day yesterday, right?"

"Well, yes, but I was in bed until the book signing. I had a real bad migraine and had to cancel my class."

"Bummer. So how was the signing? I'll bet the ladies were all over him."

"It was good and yes they all wanted a magazine signed by him."

"Did you get one?"

"Yes."

"Awesome. I want to see it when you get home."

"Okay." She eyed it on the table and smiled.

"So tell me how the party went last night. You got a photo and you must've stayed out late partying."

"I had a good time at the party. It was fun."

"That's it? No details?"

"Chyna, I want to ask you something."

"Okay. Shoot."

"Last night Nicolo invited me to join him in the morning in the hotel exercise room to work out."

"He what? You're kidding!"

"No, not kidding. And then he asked me for my room number. But this morning he didn't call and when I went to the room to exercise he wasn't there. What do you think? I probably shouldn't have given him my room number."

"How was he last night when you said goodbye? What did he say?"

"Well, I had to leave the party to drive another author back and he seemed surprised. He said leaving already?"

"Woman you blew it. He asked for your room number and then you left. That was not a smart move. You should've had some other author give her a ride. You don't even know these people and you don't owe any of them anything. You've got to stop being so damn helpful."

"But I like helping people."

"That's not the point. You missed your big chance with him

because of some author you don't even know. He wanted some booty, got your room number and then you ran out on him. You know what he did? He moved on to another woman who was happy to spend the night with him. He didn't give another thought to you and that's why he didn't show up to exercise. He probably slept in after a wild night with her."

"He's here with his mother."

"Doesn't matter. He wanted to know what room you were in didn't he? He would've come to your room. You had a slight chance. God knows why. Then you blew it."

"He did seem attentive at dinner. Like he was really interested in getting to know me. He and his mother were both so nice. I thought he was just inviting me to work out as a friend. His mother works out with him too."

"Oh. Well, you didn't tell me that. So maybe he wasn't interested in coming to your room. Maybe he really was only interested in working out with you. You're older than he is. Why would he want you when younger models and actresses surround him? Believe me honey, you're pretty but you're no model. He's in a whole different category than you are. I still say he found some young honey to spend the evening with into the wee hours."

Not interested in me? But the way he looked at me with those eyes. Those deep brown eyes that made me feel he could see into my soul. Like he could see me. Really see me. It had felt so real.

"Men are so confusing."

"Not to me. That's why you need me. Okay so you know he found some other girl to sleep with. Probably younger and prettier. And as for the gym, face it. You're really out of shape. He mentioned the gym because you need to get fitter. Be glad you didn't sleep with him. Did you really want him to see you naked the way you are right now?"

"Well, I guess not. Getting naked with him? I just met him."

"And that is why you never get laid. So what are you doing today since you don't have to drive home?"

"I'm going to write."

"Cool beans. I've got to go. Give me a call tomorrow when you get home."

"All right. Thanks Chyna."

"No problem. Later." Chyna hung up.

Jenna sat looking at her phone.

Chyna is right. Why would he be interested in me? Nicolo Maldini could have his pick of any girl he wanted. And anyway I'm not a girl any more but a grown woman. He probably likes them much younger than himself.

She got up and walked over to the floor length mirror. She let the robe drop to the floor and looked into the mirror. Her shoulders sank.

Look at you. You're overweight, have to wear push up bras for lift and your ass is huge.

She cupped her hands beneath her breasts, where they were heaviest, and lifted them. In a bra she didn't look so bad, but she was still far from those cover models with their perfect round breasts like two matching cantaloupes. She sighed.

And this belly. Rounded, not flat. Even if I lost all the extra padding, these hips would still be wide because of my bone structure. Not that any of this extra padding is going anywhere any time soon.

No, a model she was not. She could never compete with the

beautiful women Nicolo was surrounded by. It would be futile to even try.

And though she didn't look her age, as people often told her, she had to be older than he was. This was the first time she'd ever been attracted to a younger man.

But his eyes.

She kept coming back to his eyes. The memory of them stayed so strong she could close her eyes right now and see him looking at her, gazing into her eyes, wanting to know more about her.

Picking up the robe, she slid it back on and then climbed onto the bed with her laptop. Today she was going to find out more about him. Then she'd get to writing.

His site was professional and slick, as she expected a cover model's site would be. The photo gallery held a sampling of shots and poses. Handsome in every single one, the ones she liked best were the ones where he looked into the camera as if he was looking straight at her. Again it was his eyes. She'd never forget what it felt like to be beneath his gaze.

Goodness but he was handsome. And that gaze did something to her, pulled her in like a magnet. Too bad she would never see him again.

She logged off the Internet and got to work on her book. Writing in hotel rooms was always nice when they were quiet and isolated. She could order room service in the bigger hotels and not have to leave her room. Too bad she couldn't do that here, but at least she could relax in her robe and work until she had to go out for food.

After writing for several hours, the phone in her room rang. She reached over and answered it. "Hello?"

"You stayed." Nicolo's voice came through the phone, strong and clear. The deep stir within her started again with just those two words.

Jenna's stomach did a flip.

"Yes. The route home is icy so I'm staying one more night."

"Good. Join us for lunch. We're walking to the restaurant and then hanging out in my room."

Lunch. He's inviting me to lunch! Oh but with his mother, of course. Settle down girl. This is not a date. He's just being nice.

"Oh. Okay." She needed to get dressed. "Are you leaving right now?"

"As soon as you meet us in the lobby."

"Okay. I'll be down in a few minutes."

"Good. See you then." She could hear the smile in his voice.

"Yes." A huge grin crossed her face. Even if it wasn't a date she'd get to see him.

He called.

She hopped off the bed giddy but with a sense of urgency and turned to her suitcase while shrugging out of her robe, which dropped to the floor. She pulled out panties and bra and then hurried into them. Soft cotton black pants she'd have worn for the drive home and a soft blue long sleeved shirt were next. They were the only clean things she hadn't already worn. She hurried to pull her hair into a scrunchie ponytail at the back of her neck and then reached for her socks and tennis shoes. Dressed, she grabbed her purse and coat. Pausing half a second as she passed the mirror she reached a hand to her hair.

Lord help me, my hair is a mess and I don't have time for makeup.

She headed to the elevator and rode down, pulling her coat on as she rode.

Nicolo was watching for her as she stepped off the elevator. "There she is." He greeted her with a smile. "Glad you could join us."

"Me too." She smiled back at him. "Thanks for inviting me. Sorry I took so long. I'd been writing when you called."

Oh no, did I save my work? Or turn off the computer? I rushed out the door so fast. I hope I remembered to save.

Nicolo, Angela, Amy and Brett had all been waiting for her. Jenna buttoned her coat and wrapped her scarf around her neck. "Has anyone been outside yet?"

Amy answered. "The guys have. The walk to the restaurant has been shoveled."

"Oh good."

Very good as I forgot to wear my boots. Wonder what else I've forgotten?

As they walked up the hill, Nicolo walked beside her. "Did you get your workout in this morning?" he asked.

"Yes, I did, at six a.m. Real early for me. But afterward I felt great. Thank you for suggesting it. I need to do that more often when I travel.'

"You're welcome. I'm glad you had a good one. I slept past six this morning. Was up late last night."

"I wondered where you were but I had a good workout anyway."

"Good." he smiled.

They reached the restaurant, went inside and were seated.

"Hello, Penny." Jenna greeted their waitress. "How are you today?

"Just fine. How are you? Making the long drive back today?"

"I'm good. No, I'm staying another night to avoid the ice."

"I'm glad to hear it. They're saying it's ugly out there, but it's going to warm up tomorrow and start melting."

When the waitress left Nicolo looked at Jenna. "You two know each other?"

"Penny waited on me Thursday night after I arrived. She's a very sweet girl."

Nicolo gave Jenna a wide smile and she basked beneath the light in his eyes.

"You're a sweet girl yourself, Jenna Heart."

She blushed. "Thank you."

The food, the company and the conversation were so enjoyable time flew. After lunch they all headed back to Nicolo's room to watch football. The red roses were in the room on the dresser beside the TV.

Jenna looked at them and smiled.

Girlfriend, remember? He's not into you that way; he's just being friendly.

Angela who'd seen Jenna glance, said, " Aren't they beautiful? Nic gave them to me."

"Oh." Jenna's eyebrows shot up in surprise. "Yes, they are. How sweet of him."

Hmmm. So he doesn't care about the flowers. Question is, does he care about the person who sent them to him? Well, it doesn't matter. He's not into me that way.

Jenna didn't follow football, or hadn't since that ex boyfriend back in high school. But she enjoyed Nicolo's company and his enthusiasm for the games.

They ended up ordering pizzas when he found a place that would deliver for an extra charge. It took a little longer to arrive than a usual pizza delivery would, but they enjoyed the pizzas after they arrived.

Nicolo wasn't upset by the late delivery or when one of his teams lost. He didn't appear to be a man who lost his temper easily. One more thing Jenna admired about him. At one point he had looked at his phone, then turned it off and said he was taking the day off. With that, he tossed it into his suitcase, then turned his attention fully to the game and to visiting with everyone.

Too soon they all said good night and Amy and Brett went to their room while Nicolo walked Jenna back to hers.

He waited by the door as she opened it. "I had fun spending time with you Jenna."

"I enjoyed our time together too."

"Could I have your phone number? I'd like to keep in touch."

"Sure." Surprised, she rattled the number off as he put it into his phone.

He wants my number. Oh my goodness. He really wants my number. Oh but why? Why would he be interested in me?

Then he put his phone away. "Great. I'll call you to make sure you made it home safe."

"Oh, that would be nice. Thank you."

He leaned in before she had a chance to say another word and brushed his lips against hers in a soft kiss. And with that kiss, the whys and the words went completely out of her head. There was only this moment, this kiss.

She kissed him back, closing her eyes, filled with the gentleness of the kiss and the way his lips felt against hers. She leaned slightly forward toward him as if drawn by an invisible thread. And when he stopped, pulling away with a smile and said, "I'd like to see you again, Jenna," she could hardly believe it was she, Jenna Heart being kissed by Nicolo Maldini.

He wants to see me again.

"Yes," her voice came out breathy, "I'd like that."

"Good. We'll make arrangements. Once you're home safe. Sweet dreams, Jenna Heart."

"Sweet dreams." She stood reluctantly not wishing to close the door, wanting to prolong their moments together.

He bent down to give her one more soft kiss and then he gave her a grin. "Good night sweet Jenna."

"Good night." Her words came out soft, whisper like.

He turned and walked down the hall and she closed the door so he wouldn't think she was watching him walk away. Though a man with a body like that was probably used to women staring at his glutes. Still, this was Nicolo. Her friend. Possibly her new boyfriend, if she was dreaming.

He kissed me.

She leaned against the door and pressed her fingertips to her lips as if to seal the kiss and the way it felt. The kiss was like a dream she wanted to remember so she tried to capture it before it drifted away.

* * * *

Chyna's call that night was the worst call Jenna had ever taken from a friend. The moment Chyna heard Nicolo had kissed Jenna she started in.

"Of course he kissed you."

Why does she sound so disgusted?

"Don't you know Italian men are masters at seduction? They'll kiss any woman they can get their hands on. Don't read too much into that kiss. They make terrible husbands. Always seducing the next woman. So you'd better keep that in mind before he breaks your heart."

"No, he's not that way." Jenna wanted to stop this conversation. She wanted to stay in the soft, floating, happy feeling Nicolo's kiss had left her in. Chyna was ruining everything.

Why does Chyna have to be so negative about Nicolo and me? Why isn't she being supportive?

"He's very nice and he even asked for my phone number and said he wanted us to get together again."

"Girl, men like him pick up women wherever they go. You were just convenient. Now that you're not convenient, he's already forgotten about you. Just because he asked for your phone number doesn't mean he'll call."

"Well I believe he will."

"You didn't sleep with him, did you?"

"No."

"Then why would he call? You live in totally different states and it would be too much effort for the two of you to get together."

Jenna was quiet thinking.

If he actually makes the effort so we can see each other again, then that would mean he really does like me. Because we do live far away from each other.

"You're day dreaming about him aren't you?"

"Yes."

"He's fine for a fantasy, but in real life it'll never happen. You ought to be glad it won't. You won't have to go through the embarrassment of him seeing you naked."

Why does she keep bringing that up? This conversation needs to stop. Now.

She interrupted. "Chyna, I have a long drive tomorrow. I need to get to sleep."

"Okay. Night girlfriend. Call me when you get home."

"Night." Jenna hung up.

Why do I always feel deflated somehow after I talk to her? And why can't she be happy for me? This is not how friends are supposed to act.

Jenna got ready for bed, pulled down the covers, climbed in and then started on her thankful list.

One, Nicolo called my room. Two, Nicolo invited me to lunch and then football and pizza. Hanging out with him was fun. Three, Nicolo asked for my number. Four, Nicolo kissed me. Five, Nicolo wants to see me again. He said so. So he must want to.

Every one of my five thankful things is about Nicolo. Well that's just fine because this has been one of the happiest days of my life.

She drifted off to sleep and slept like a baby.

* * * *

The following day the drive home was uneventful. She didn't see Nicolo and his mother again. Her night had been full of dreams of Nicolo kissing her. She looked for them when she was ready to check out but they were already gone.

The bad weather had stopped, the ice melted and the road crews had helped it along. Driving along, only happy thoughts filled her mind. This time when a song repeated one too many times on the radio, she turned it off and hummed. Silence was more peaceful and she wanted to stay in the happy state she'd been in since spending yesterday with Nicolo. He was on her mind throughout the long drive.

How long will it take him to call me?

CHAPTER FOUR

Jenna was home safe and settled back in with all the doors locked and lights on. Her phone rang. Chyna had called twice earlier but Jenna had ignored the calls. This number wasn't one she knew, but she decided to answer. "Hello?"

"Hello, Jenna." Nicolo's deep sexy voice poured through the phone making her giddy as a schoolgirl.

"Hello." So excited to hear from him, she squeaked the word.

"Did you make it home safe?"

"Yes, I did. And you and your mother?"

"We're both home safe as well."

"Good." She paused. "I'm glad we waited that extra day."

"I'm glad too. So when are we going to see each other again?"

"I don't know. You probably have a busy schedule."

"Not so much around Christmas. I keep that time clear for family."

"That's nice. If they're all like your mama, it sounds wonderful."

"You should come to New Jersey. Visit. Have you ever been to Atlantic City?"

"No, I haven't ever been."

"Then come. I'll show you around."

"You'd find me boring."

"Why would you say that?"

"Because I'm too shy. If I'm at a party, I get too quiet. I'm not out on the dance floor partying like most girls. Chyna is always trying to drag me to clubs and I run out of excuses and reasons to turn her down. But the truth is, I really don't like bars or clubs and I'm not much of a partier. So I'm not sure I'd like Atlantic City."

"I'm not into partying, bars, or clubs either. I'd show you other parts of Atlantic City. Take you to the good restaurants, see the boardwalk and watch the ocean. Have fun."

It did sound like fun. And this was Nicolo. She'd be happy if he took her anywhere and fed her nothing but peanut butter and jelly sandwiches.

"That sounds nice."

"It will be. Say you'll come."

"You're constantly surprising me. You're not at all like the actors in People magazine. They're always photographed coming out of some club or party. I thought you might be like that too."

"Nope. I'm just me. What you see is what you get."

"Well, I will think about it."

"You do that, Jenna. Get settled in, have a good night's sleep and I'll call you later. I'm glad you're home safe."

"Me too. Thank you Nicolo. I'm glad you called to check on me."

"Of course. Well, you get some rest and have sweet dreams, sweet girl."

"Thank you Nicolo. You have sweet dreams too. Good night."

"Good night Jenna."

* * * *

One week passed and then Nicolo was asking again. One week during which Jenna had taken only one of Chyna's calls. Beyond the first few seconds of welcome home, Chyna switched to how Jenna needed to get back to reality and stop dreaming about Nicolo because she was so far beneath him. After that call Jenna was done. She didn't need all that negativity poured into her ear, especially from one who was supposed to be her friend. She'd ignored two calls from her former friend and critique partner, but this time it was Nicolo on the phone and she answered.

"Jenna, come spend Christmas with me," Nicolo said. "My mom always makes a big Italian style Christmas dinner and feeds the whole family."

"Oh, Nicolo, I don't know. It's a long way to drive and you'll be with your family."

"I'll fly you out. You don't have to drive. In fact, I don't want you to drive. I don't want you getting stuck on the road, breaking down, or driving in bad weather. I want to know you're safe. Fly out and join me. Say yes."

"But Nicolo… tickets this time of year are so expensive."

"I don't care. It's not a problem for me. Stop worrying about that. I'm sending you a ticket."

"I just don't want to be in the way."

"You won't be in the way. My family would love to have you here. My mom loves to cook and the more people she can cook for, the happier she is. We both want you to come. Say yes."

"Well, I… I just don't know what to say." Tears brimmed in her eyes and she knew if she said any more he'd hear it in her voice.

"Say yes."

"Yes Nicolo." Her words were almost a whisper, she was so choked up. "I'd love to."

He wanted her to come for Christmas. Maybe Santa was granting her wish this year.

She smiled. She was much too old to believe in Santa, but maybe there was some sort of Christmas magic at work because this seemed like a dream. If it was, she didn't want to wake up.

* * * *

Jenna's connecting flight from Atlanta landed in New Jersey and passengers prepared to disembark. Jenna stood to get her carryon out of the overhead compartment. It was heavy and the man behind her helped her to pull it down.

"Thank you," she said.

"You're welcome and Merry Christmas," he said.

"Merry Christmas."

Thanks to Nicolo, she'd found her Christmas spirit and she was looking forward to the holiday.

In the days leading up to her flight, Nicolo kept reassuring her by the things he said that both he and his mother really did want Jenna to join them for Christmas. He'd asked a lot of questions about how she and her mother had celebrated the holidays and it did her good to talk about it, though she became emotional each time. He'd taken her emotional state in stride and made comments, which cheered her.

She rolled her suitcase along behind and waited by the cockpit as the people in front of her stepped off. The crew had a festive air, as did everyone on the plane. She smiled and took a deep breath before stepping off onto the ramp.

Well, this is it. I'm here now.

New Jersey was colder than Memphis and snow was falling. Jenna shivered and her nerves kicked in again. This was the most impulsive thing she'd ever done, flying to another state to be with a man she'd just met. But this was it. She was doing it. She squared her shoulders and rolled her carry on up the ramp into the airport. As she came through the doorway feeling shy and unsure of herself, she saw him.

Nicolo stood watching for her with such a welcoming smile on his face she couldn't help but feel his warmth.

It's Beginning to Look a Lot Like Christmas played over the speaker system. Jenna felt like humming the peppy song and her giddy grin was as wide as the sky.

Jenna walked over to Nicolo and stood looking up at him with a silly grin. "I made it."

"Yes, you did." His voice and his smile covered her with warmth while his deep brown eyes took her in.

"Thank you for the tickets and for inviting me to your home to be with your family."

"You're welcome, Jenna. I'm glad you came." He wrapped her in a warm enveloping hug and happiness welled up inside of her while his strong arms held her.

Home.

Crazy it might be, but wrapped in his arms, she felt a sense of coming home.

"I'm glad too."

He gave her another squeeze and then let her go.

"I don't have any checked luggage."

"Is that all you brought?" He pointed to her carryon.

"Yes. I tend to travel light."

"All right then. " Nicolo took hold of her carryon with one hand and reached for her hand with the other.

Holding hands all the way through the airport, Jenna kept thinking, this is really happening. Nicolo is holding my hand and everyone can see.

She felt as if she could float. Outside of the airport snow fell, the powder covering everything. Nicolo continued to hold her hand until they were outside and then he said, "Do you have gloves?"

"Oh, yes. Yes I do." She reached into her coat pockets, pulled them out and put them on.

Taking her gloved hand again they headed for the parking garage where he led her to a red Corvette.

"Oh, is she yours? She's beautiful," Jenna said.

"Yes, she's mine," Nicolo said. "I like her." He winked. Then he opened the car door for Jenna, helped her in and then loaded her carryon into the car. Getting into the driver's seat he said, "Do you want to go straight to your hotel or do you want to stop somewhere along the way?"

"Let's go straight to the hotel. I need to freshen up after spending all day in airports and planes."

"Then that's where we're headed. You can rest and take a nap and I'll take you out for a late dinner after you wake up."

"That sounds good. Thank you Nicolo. You've been so good to me."

"Can't imagine why anyone wouldn't be good to you, Jenna. You're a sweetheart."

She relaxed into her seat as Nicolo drove the corvette away from the airport to her hotel. This hotel had a pool, a hot tub, and a restaurant. She wouldn't have to leave her hotel unless she wanted to. This was how she liked to travel because so often she wrote when she was traveling and it made it easier.

"How is your writing going? Will you need to do any writing on this trip?"

"It's going well. I'm not under any deadlines so I don't have to. But I like writing. It's not just something I do as a job to make money. If I go for too many days without writing, my happiness level tends to fall."

"Well, I want you to be happy so if you need to write on this trip, then do it. Did you bring your laptop?"

"Yes, it's in my carryon. I wrote some on both flights though so I'm good for a while."

"Good." He smiled.

He pulled up to her hotel, went inside with her to get her checked in and then he said, "All right sweet girl. Get some rest and call me when you wake up. Then we'll go to dinner."

"Thank you, Nicolo. That sounds lovely."

He lifted her hand and kissed it. "Until tonight then."

She smiled and blushed. "Yes, tonight."

He waited until she'd walked to the elevator and got in before he turned and left.

All the way to her room Jenna wondered just what she could have done to get so lucky. It seemed Santa might just be granting her wish this year.

The room was restful and quiet, so she pulled off her clothes, got a warm shower and then climbed into bed for a nap. It was late when she woke. The room was dark and she rolled over to look at the clock. Eight thirty p.m.

Oh no. I slept so late. Nicolo has to be hungry.

She picked up the phone and dialed his number.

"Hello, sleeping beauty. Did you sleep well?"

"Yes, I did. But Nicolo, I feel terrible about sleeping so long when you were waiting to have dinner. I'm so sorry."

"Nothing to be sorry about. Are you hungry? Ready for me to come get you?"

"Yes, if you still want to. I am hungry."

"I'm on my way."

"Thank you Nicolo."

"You're welcome. Be thinking about what you'd like to eat. Seafood, Italian or something else."

"Okay."

She got dressed and went downstairs to wait for him. It wasn't long before he pulled up in front of the hotel. She went out the door as he was getting out of his car. He opened the car door for her and she got in then he went around to his side.

He's so polite and thoughtful and his manners are old-world gentleman. Oh, how I like that. I would be so spoiled if I ever got used to this.

"So what are you hungry for?"

"Well, I love seafood and in Memphis we are nowhere near an ocean."

"I love seafood too and know the perfect place."

He made a quick phone call and then started the car. They cruised along until they reached the restaurant and he pulled into the nearly empty parking lot.

"Are you sure we aren't too late for dinner? I slept a long time."

"It's okay Jenna. They know me. And they're expecting us."

"Oh good."

Again he opened the door for her and then with small touches on her elbow and back guided her into the restaurant.

Dark woods and white tablecloths set the cozy and elegant atmosphere as candles flickered on the tables sending out a romantic glow. They would almost have the place to themselves. Only one other couple was dining and lingering over dessert.

"Nic!" a large hearty man boomed out. "Good to see you. And who is this lovely lady with you tonight?"

"Joe, this is Jenna. Jenna, this is Joe, one of my oldest friends."

"A pleasure." Joe took hold of Jenna's hand and kissed it. "Beautiful lady. Welcome."

They shed their coats and were seated. Nicolo's cell phone rang.

He took it out of his pocket, glanced at it and frowned.

"If you need to take that, I don't mind, " she said.

"No, it's nothing." He ignored the call and placed his phone on the table face down. "Let's enjoy our dinner."

Joe brought out a good bottle of wine with his compliments and poured a glass for her. It was clear from the way he spoke to Nicolo, calling him Nic and from the special treatment, that Joe and Nicolo were good friends from a long way back.

"Now what will you two have?" Joe said.

"I'd like the shrimp scampi," Jenna said. "I love seafood. There isn't much good seafood to be had in Memphis. It has to be shipped in. Plenty of barbeque though."

Nicolo hadn't even looked at the menu. He handed it back to Joe. "That sounds good. I'll have the same."

Nic's phone vibrated on the table. Zzzt zzzt. He ignored it.

"Very good " Joe nodded. "I'll bring you shrimp cocktail and an antipasta plate to enjoy while you wait. Bread will be out of the oven soon."

"Sounds wonderful." Jenna said with a smile. As Joe walked back to the kitchen, she said. "He's such a nice man. And the food sounds delicious. I'm glad you brought me here tonight."

"I'm glad too. I'm going to enjoy showing you around my hometown. So, Jenna Heart, what are you most looking forward to this Christmas?"

"Spending the holiday with you and your family. I can't tell you how much this means to me, Nicolo. Do you prefer Nicolo or Nic?"

"Either is fine with me, sweetheart. Which ever you want." He smiled. "I had to use all my powers of persuasion to convince you to come. I'm glad you said yes."

"Well, I had just met you and I can be shy sometimes."

"Just sometimes?" he laughed.

"Well, more often than not." she giggled.

He grinned deeper. "I can tell that about you. I love to hear you giggle."

Zzzt zzzt. The phone vibrated again.

"Do you need to get that?" she asked. "I really don't mind."

"No. It's not important right now." He leaned forward and reached his hand out to her. She placed her hand in his. His gaze was only on her and it was clear he was showing her that she was important right now, not his phone. She had his full attention.

"I can hardly believe I'm here with you," she said. Her stomach rumbled.

"Sounds like you're a hungry lady." Joe placed the shrimp cocktail in front of them along with an antipasta plate as they released each other's hands.

"It looks delicious. Thank you." She'd almost finished her glass of wine before the food came and was feeling a bit tipsy. "I haven't had much to eat today. Everything looks so good."

"We'll have you full and happy before you leave," Joe said. "If you want anything else, you just ask."

"Yes, I will. Thank you."

Joe nodded and walked back to the kitchen as Nic refilled her wine glass. When he handed it to her she said, "I keep wanting to pinch myself to see if this is real."

"This is real." He reached his hand out toward her. "Want me to pinch you?"

She started giggling. "No."

His voice teased and he grinned deeper. "Are you sure?" He moved his index finger and thumb in a pinching motion. "Just a little pinch? To prove you're not dreaming."

Jenna shook her head no and giggled again.

The bell over the door jangled as another customer came in. A woman wrapped in a black coat and red scarf, which covered part of her face, stood inside looking around the restaurant. They both glanced over at her.

Nic pulled back his hand, the smile and the tease in his voice gone. "I won't pinch you unless you want me to."

Why had his playful mood vanished? Have I done something wrong?

Joe hurried out from the back and he and Nicolo exchanged glances which seemed to communicate something, though Jenna didn't know what. Joe went to the front of the restaurant to greet the woman. Low voices were all Jenna could hear. The woman's voice rose with each word.

"Well, you just tell him that!" She stood with her hands on her curvy hips.

He crossed his arms across his chest. Standing with feet shoulder's width apart Joe made a formidable sight. "Leave. Now."

"I'll go. But you tell him." The woman spun and rushed out the door.

Joe shook his head and then unfolded his arms, turned and headed to their table. "How are you two doing?"

"We're fine," Nicolo said. "How is dinner coming?"

"Coming right up. I just wanted to…" Joe glanced at Jenna and then clammed up.

"We're good," Nic said. "Just hungry."

Joe nodded and went off to the kitchen.

"I wonder what that woman wanted?" Jenna looked toward the window but could see nothing but snow coming down outside. "Do you suppose he told her the kitchen was closed this late?"

"Who knows? Some women get upset easy."

"I don't. It takes a lot for me to get upset."

He rolled his shoulders releasing tension. She enjoyed the way his body moved, all those strong muscles drawing her gaze.

"Maybe once you've had something to eat this evening will seem less dream like. Are you feeling all right? You mentioned you were light headed in the car."

"Yes, I am lightheaded and I do need to eat. But that's not it. I feel like I've stepped into a dream and I keep wondering why someone like you would ever be attracted to someone like me."

"Jenna." He took her hand. "Why do you keep saying things like that? Do you not know how beautiful you are?"

She blushed and looked down at their hands upon the white tablecloth. His, strong and tanned. Hers, soft and pale. His hand was so warm and real.

"You are beautiful, Jenna. Genuine, not plastic like other women. I see all these nipped, tucked, enhanced and made up women in my work. They begin to look alike. You," he moved his hand away from hers and reached out and touched her chin lightly before brushing long silky strands of hair behind her ear, "are beautiful just as you are. Don't change a thing."

The warmth of his words and his touch soaked in and filled her heart with joy and wonder. It did seem like a dream, but it wasn't. This was real. She really was here having dinner with Nic and she felt like the most adored woman in the world.

She wasn't sure what to say, but when she looked up into his dark brown eyes, hers were full of tears of joy.

He gave her a warm smile, which made her feel a glow like the candlelight flickering on the table. "Do you remember when I asked you to join us for lunch?"

"Yes, I remember every moment of that weekend."

"Many women would have kept me waiting while they primped and fussed putting on makeup and doing their hair. Not thinking about the others they kept waiting. But you, there you were coming off of that elevator, with your hair thrown into a ponytail, a fresh scrubbed face and wearing that beautiful smile. I knew then I wanted to spend more time with you."

"Oh. Well, I didn't want to keep anyone waiting. That wouldn't have been very nice and I knew you all were probably as hungry as I was."

"And there it is. That inner beauty I see shining through in everything you do. The way you think of others. The way you remembered the waitress's name. Do you know how rare that is?"

"Well, I know it's strange. Chyna has told me often enough how weird and unnecessary it is, always using everyone's names."

"Then your friend does not understand you or see you as I do. She doesn't see people the way you do. Really see people instead of being so self focused."

"That's probably true. She was always trying to get me to be more like her."

"Don't be. I like you the way you are. Do you think you can do something for me?"

"I would try... depending on what it is."

"Stop thinking that you aren't good enough. Because you are beautiful just as you are. Inner beauty is what matters most and you are such a beautiful person, both inside and out. Every time I see you, every time I talk to you, I'm reminded of that. Any man would be lucky to have you. I'm lucky that you're here with me tonight having dinner."

"Oh, Nicolo... I don't know what to say."

Joe brought out their dinner plates and placed them on the table. Observing their conversation, he didn't say a word, but stepped aside.

"Then don't say anything. Just enjoy your dinner." Nic picked up his fork.

"All right. I can do that."

For the rest of the evening he talked about growing up on the Jersey shore and about all the places he wanted to show her before she went home again. Jenna relaxed as she ate and laughed. The evening flew by and soon he was driving her back to the hotel and they were saying their good nights.

He leaned in to kiss her. His hands slipped around her pulling her close as their lips met. Her hands slipped around the back of his neck. The kiss began light as before, his lips gentle upon hers, drawing her into a longer kiss as her lips parted, letting him in. His kiss coaxed her like no other as her whole body responded, closer and closer. She moaned. He kissed her deeper and then pulled away, both of them coming up for air, both smiling.

She caught a breath and then her words came out breathy. "I had a wonderful evening, Nicolo. Thank you."

He touched his fingertip to her lips, running across them, leaving behind a tingle. "There's something else I've noticed about you."

"What's that?" She smiled beneath the touch of his fingertip, speaking slowly, still in the glow of their kiss.

"You are thankful all the time, for even the smallest of things. I like that about you."

"Thank you Nicolo." The words were out before she realized what she was saying. She giggled. "I did it again."

"Yes," he laughed. "You did."

"Must be a habit," she laughed.

"It's a good one. Don't ever lose it."

"I won't." She wouldn't tell him yet about her thankful list she did every night. Because he might ask her what was on it and she didn't want him to know that lately it had been all about him. Tonight's list would be easy because of him.

"Good night Jenna."

"Good night Nicolo."

She waited while he walked to the elevator and then closed and locked her door. She spent the rest of the evening floating on a happy cloud and remembering everything he'd said and the way he'd kissed her. It was one of the happiest days of her life.

* * * *

Nic called Joe as he drove away from the hotel. "What did Ember want?"

"She wanted to come in and talk to you, but I discouraged her."

"Thanks, Joe."

"She also wanted me to give you a message."

"I can only imagine."

"She said to tell you if you sleep with that girl, you'll wish you hadn't. That girl is nuts, Nic. She has crazy eyes. Crazy Embers. Be careful she don't set fires on you."

"Ha! That's a good name for her. She's got some problems. I wish she'd get help but she refuses to see anyone. There's not much I can do for her. Thanks for handling her, keeping her away from Jenna and keeping it quiet."

"Any time, Nic, you know that. Jenna is a sweet one. I'm glad you brought her by. Is it serious with this one?"

"We're just having fun getting to know each other."

"First time you brought one of your girls around for the holidays with the family. Everyone is going to be asking."

"Yeah, I know. They can ask. She is a sweet girl. But we'll see where it goes. I'm not looking to settle down. If the right one comes along? Sure. Til then, I'm having fun."

"This one could be the right one, Nic. She's the kind you marry, not the kind you play around with. Be careful she ain't more serious than you are. You want me to give crazy Embers a message for you? Keep her from setting any fires?"

"Thanks, Joe. I can handle her."

"If you need me, call."

"I will. Night, Joe."

"Night."

Nic hung up and thought about the events of the evening.

Ember Morten. Crazy Embers. He shook his head.

Joe would nickname you quickly if you didn't have one already. That poor girl did need help. Too bad she wouldn't listen and get it. I won't to allow her to ruin Jenna's visit. Sweet Jenna. He smiled thinking of her.

When he got home he sat looking at the phone calls and text messages Ember had sent. Her tone had changed as she'd grown angrier and she'd basically blown up his phone all night. She'd seen him go into the restaurant with Jenna and that had really set her off.

He deleted the messages with a frown. *Talking to her had done no good. Ignoring her hadn't either so far. If she continued this way, he'd have to do something about it.*

CHAPTER FIVE

Jenna had just climbed out of the hot tub at the hotel the next day when her phone dinged with a text from Nic.

Good morning, sweet girl. I hope you slept well.

She wrapped the towel around her and sat on a lounge chair before texting back.

Good morning. Yes, I did. I hope you did too.

I did, thanks. What are your plans for the day?

After I get a shower I thought I'd write for a few hours.

Okay. Want to go with me to visit a couple kids?

Whose kids are you visiting and where?

I'll call you.

The phone rang and she answered. "Hello?"

"I'd much rather hear your voice."

"Me too. Hear yours, I mean."

"The kids, Katy and Brian. They're both cancer patients. Katy is in the hospital and Brian is at home now. I'd planned to take them some treats and surprise them."

"Oh, Nic. That's so sweet. Of course I'd love to come, if I won't be in the way."

"You're never in the way, sweetheart. Can you be ready by two? We'll spend at least an hour with each of them."

"Yes, of course. I'm glad you invited me Nic. Thank you."

"You're welcome. See you at two. Happy writing."

"Thank you, yes see you at two."

"Better get to work now."

"Okay." Still she hovered on the phone not wanting to hang up. She hated to say goodbye to him. What was this? Silly as a schoolgirl with a crush, she giggled.

"Go write. I'll be coming for you soon."

She giggled again. "Okay."

"Bye Jenna."

"Bye Nic."

He hung up and she sat there wrapped in her towel, holding the cell phone with a silly smile on her face. After a few minutes of rerunning what he'd said through her head, she got up, pulled on her cover up and headed to back to her room. She would shower and write for several hours then have a nap after lunch so she'd be rested when Nic picked her up. It would be another perfect day.

Nic called about twenty minutes after she'd finished her nap. Just enough time to freshen up and be downstairs to meet him.

Ever the gentleman, he held doors for her again and soon they were driving off in his corvette. His car was full of surprises for the children and he was as energized as she'd ever seen him. It was clear this was something he loved to do.

He pulled into the hospital parking lot and then she helped him carry the bags in. The first child they visited, a girl named Katy who was twelve, had been undergoing chemo and had lost all her hair. She looked so thin and ill in her hospital bed but her face lit up the moment she saw Nicolo enter the room.

His enthusiasm was infectious and everyone in the room caught it. Jenna felt she was witnessing a very special and private moment and she was honored that he had asked her to join him.

This was the real Nicolo Maldini and he was as beautiful inside as he was outside.

It was a gift to see him like this, to be here with him. Her heart was so full and her eyes teared up but she blinked the tears away and smiled.

Nic was right. I see people differently than most and he sees this because he sees people the same way I do. He notices things. He sees the people around him and wants to be kind and helpful. He's bringing such joy to this girl. The love in this room is so beautiful.

Her heart was full and she was falling fast, fast as a shooting star, head over heels in love with Nicolo Maldini.

The second child they visited was a boy named Brian who was ten and who had been in a terrible car accident and lost the use of his right arm. He was home now with a right arm that ended above his elbow and he had to adjust to his new life as he learned to use his left. He and Nic talked football. Nic had brought him a nerf football and was working with him on catching it with his left. It was clear the boy looked up to Nic like he was his hero.

Jenna had to admit to herself that he was looking like a hero to her too. The image of Nic handing out gifts made her see him in a different light than that of a cover model.

He's like Santa. How did I never put that together before this moment? Nic, like Saint Nic. But no, this is more than gifts for children. Nicolo Maldini is more like Santa and an angel rolled into one. Because he gives beyond presents. He gives of himself.

The gifts Nic had given these children were more than the surprises he'd picked out. The gifts of his time and his love and his words of encouragement would linger long after the surprises had gone. And the memory of sharing these wonderful moments with him would linger with her long after she went home.

When they got in the car to leave, her turned to her with a grin and said, "This is what I live for."

Watching him and still feeling full of emotion, her eyes teared up and she said, "I can see how much this means to you and to the children. Thank you for letting me share in this very special day. I'm honored you wanted me to come along."

She was blinking away her teary eyes when his hand closed over hers. "I'm glad you came with me, Jenna." He gave her hand a squeeze. "Now, how about we go get a pizza? I'm starving."

She laughed. "Okay Nic. That sounds good."

He released her hand and started to drive. "I know the perfect place."

* * * *

The next morning she'd just gotten out of the pool and dried off when a text from Nic came in.

Come for dinner. My place tonight. I'll cook you a wonderful Italian meal.

The text popped into her phone and she sat on a lounge chair to catch her breath. Laying back she closed her eyes. The phone rang again. Thinking it was Nicolo she answered without looking at it.

"Hello," she said with a smile in her voice.

"You're sounding happy," Chyna said. "What's going on over there?"

"Oh, plenty of things."

"I have news about my last book. It's been nominated for a Hearts Afire award."

"Congratulations. I've always thought that was your best one."

"I'm so excited about it." Chyna then went on to tell her all about it and when she had wound down she said, "So what's going on with you?"

"Nicolo just invited me to his house for dinner."

"That might be difficult seeing as he lives so far away."

"Not really because I'm in New Jersey now."

"You're what?"

"Yes, I flew out and I'm spending the holidays out here. So I won't be able to go to lunch with you to celebrate this time, but enjoy."

There was silence on the line for a minute. For once she'd shocked Chyna.

"Well good for you getting out there and into the dating scene again. What exactly did he say when he invited you for dinner?"

"He said come to dinner at my place and I'll cook you a homemade Italian meal."

"The man can cook? Oh, that is hot," Chyna said. "That means he has domestic skills on top of all his hotness. He's creative. How many guys offer that? Wow. And he wants to get you into his house. Into his house, Jenna."

"I'm sure he has a lovely house."

"That is a total panty dropper move any time a guy wants to get you into his house. Didn't you know that?"

"Maybe he's just a nice guy who enjoys having people over to see his great house."

"The great something he wants to show you is not his house. Think about it. He's going to seduce you. So he greets you at the door, in his apron, wearing that sexy smile. Tantalizing scents are coming from the kitchen. And it's all for you. The lights are low, candles are lit, there's a bottle of wine. He brings you in, pours you a glass, and all you have to do is watch him cook, watching that sexy body while the music plays low. You start to feel warm and pampered. You have another glass of wine and feel warmer. You're halfway to having those panties off before you ever taste the first bite of your dinner."

"Chyna, I think you should be writing that scene in your next book. It's really good. But, seriously, I think he's just inviting me for dinner. It's a sweet thing to do."

"Seriously? You are totally clueless."

"I am not clueless. He's not offering this to get something. He's not that way."

"If you pay no attention to anything else I am saying to you, pay attention to this. Do not go to his house for dinner unless you plan to drop those panties."

"All right Chyna. I get it. Enough."

"I just worry about you sometimes. Know what you are doing with this guy. He's an actor. He's smooth and he'll put the moves on you once you're in that house. But that doesn't mean he wants a relationship with you. Think about how many women he's had. How many he's probably schmoozed with his romantic dinners."

"Okay. Enough. We are not discussing my love life. You know what you ought to do? You ought to include that scene you painted in one of your books."

I am done with her telling me what I should do. Done.

"Hey, you know I think I could do that with the new one I started yesterday."

And then Chyna was off and running, enthusiastic about her new story.

Good. Jenna smiled.

Fastest way to get her to change the subject is to get Chyna talking about herself and her writing. Things are much better when we stick to the subject of books. In particular, the subject of Chyna's books.

She doesn't get to hear any more about my personal life because she cannot be a supportive friend.

Finally Chyna got off the phone and Jenna was left with her thoughts.

But is Chyna right about Nicolo? It doesn't feel like it fits what I know about him, but I've only known him for a weekend and a few phone calls. Maybe he does go through women like the morning news. New today and old news passed over tomorrow. But there's only one way to find out. And that is to say yes.

And it felt right. Despite what Chyna or anyone else thinks about it.

I'm in love with Nicolo and it feels right. So how could that be wrong?

Unless he is not in love with me. I'm falling for him and he could break my heart. But I have to take that chance. I have to follow my heart.

Jenna looked forward to having dinner with Nicolo and to seeing his house if he wanted to show it off to her. Best of all he wanted to spend time with her. The giddy feeling inside of her returned the moment she pushed the conversation with Chyna out of her mind and texted back.

Yes I'd love to come to dinner at your house. Thank you Nicolo.

* * * *

She insisted on taking a taxi. It was the closest they'd come to an argument since she'd met him. He thought she was being silly and didn't understand why she wouldn't let him take care of picking her up and dropping her off.

But this way she'd have her own way to and from his house and she could call a cab any time she wanted to leave. In case Chyna was right. In case this stopped feeling right and started feeling wrong. This was the safer, smarter thing to do. She really did not know him that well. If she felt like she needed to leave, she could just go. This was leaving the door open for her to run like she had at the Christmas party. But she needed that door to be open. Just in case.

Nicolo greeted her at his front door, not wearing an apron like Chyna had painted in her imagination, but in a dark blue shirt and dark pants. "Hello, Jenna. I'm glad you came. Come in." He let her in and took her coat. "Welcome to my home."

"Hello, Nicolo. Thank you for inviting me. What a lovely home you have."

"Come into the kitchen while I finish cooking."

She followed him through the living room and into the dining room. The lights were low, the table set for two with two candles and an open bottle of wine in the middle.

Aromas coming from the kitchen made her want to close her eyes. Garlic, onions, tomato sauce, all the best of a homemade Italian sauce. While at the same time, Nicolo's gaze held her entranced. His eyes captivated her as they had that first weekend. They were the same deep brown eyes she dreamed of every night now when she slept.

"Can I do anything to help?"

"No. You just relax. Would you like a glass of wine?"

"Yes, please."

Soft music was playing. Brian McKnight. Jenna relaxed and felt herself unwinding as Nicolo poured her a glass of red wine.

"It smells delicious. What's for dinner?"

"Chicken Parm, ravioli, meatballs, Italian bread, salad and for dessert, cannoli."

"What a feast! And you've cooked all this yourself?"

"Everything except the bread and the cannoli." He smiled and handed her the glass. "For you."

Jenna beamed in return, accepted the glass and said, "Thank you."

"Come on in and make yourself comfortable."

She followed him into the kitchen. Sauce was bubbling in a pot and he turned water on to boil. Jenna settled on a chair in the kitchen and watched him work. The way the muscles in his back and arms moved were as beautiful as a dance. There was strength, contained power and grace to each movement. He reached for the knife and began to chop vegetables.

The warm house, the soft music playing and the way he spoke to her and was cooking for her made her feel warm and cared for.

Chyna is wrong. Nic isn't a man who takes, He's a man who gives and who cares.

He made her feel cherished and taken care of.

She watched the deft way his fingers moved, their dexterity and the professional way he handled the knife and placed the vegetables just so.

He was comfortable in the kitchen, experienced at cooking. As she watched his fingers move she couldn't help but wonder how his fingers might feel against her skin, how his practiced hands would guide her right to the perfect…

"Oh!"

She'd accidentally bumped her elbow and her wine glass spilled red wine onto her cream colored blouse. Red, wet speckled spots of wine covered her left breast.

He turned immediately at her cry and was now by her side holding a damp dishcloth. "Here. Let me help."

She allowed him to dab at the spots on her blouse, her breath coming quicker as his hand pressed gently against her breast but with enough pressure to sop up the spill.

The way her thoughts had been headed before she spilled her wine and his sudden nearness raised her body temperature and the yes come touch me responses her body was now giving out.

He gazed down at her and smiled, his eyes telling her he was aware of her response. "Too bad about the blouse. Though it might be saved if you took it off. Rinsing it could save it."

"I, I…" her mind went blank as her body was screaming yes, yes, take it off right now. *Touch me.* Her heartbeat raced and her breath froze. Overwhelmed she stood speechless.

He laughed and backed up, giving her more space. "Relax. It's your choice."

She took a breath releasing some tension. "Well, I guess you're right." She blushed and reaching for the top button, began to undo it.

His gaze followed her hands.

Halfway down the row of buttons, she stood and began to pull the blouse out of her skirt. She took in his expression, her eyes widening.

He's as turned on by watching my fingers as I am watching his. Could he be wondering how my fingers will feel against his skin?

He held out his hand for the blouse. "I'll take that to the laundry room and soak it."

"Yes. Thank you." Her voice did that breathy thing again.

She shrugged out of the blouse and placed it in his hands. Standing in front of him in her white lace bra she felt the blush creep over more of her body.

"Very pretty," he said.

She glanced down at the tips of her nipples, a dusty rose color through the lace, now getting harder beneath his gaze.

"If you're uncomfortable, I can lend you a t-shirt or you can stay like this." His gaze and his voice deepened. "I'd much prefer you to stay..." he smiled, "...like this."

"I'll stay." she breathed the words out.

"Good." He smiled again. "Stay." He carried her blouse off to the laundry room.

She stood right where he left her, getting her breath back under control and calming down.

He was back within a few minutes. "I put it in to soak with stain remover."

"Thank you."

"You're welcome. Let me refill your glass."

"I promise not to spill this one."

"You go ahead and spill all you want." He laughed and then his eyes moved over her slowly. "I like the view." he winked. "In fact, you could spill your wine at every dinner and I wouldn't mind a bit."

She smiled, blushing again; glad he was teasing her now, lightening the mood.

He turned back to the stove to finish cooking dinner.

Sipping her wine and watching him she thought about how close she already was to dropping her panties. Beneath his gaze it wouldn't take much. But that would be moving much too fast for her. She hoped they would take things slow.

Once he was done he turned to Jenna. "Dinner is ready."

"Good. It all smells delicious."

He came over to her and put his arm around her and led her to the dining room table. Then he pulled out her chair for her and she sat.

He bent and kissed the side of her neck.

Tingles spread through her body.

"I've been wanting to do that." His hands settled on her shoulders. "You're tense."

"Yes, well I've never eaten dinner dressed like this."

"If you change your mind and want my t-shirt, I will get it. You just say the word. Though I much prefer you like this." His warm hand moved across the back of her neck and she leaned into it and looked up at him.

"I'll stay like this."

"Then relax." His hands settled on her shoulders and he massaged them, just enough to get her shoulders to settle back down from climbing up near her ears.

He served meatballs as an appetizer followed by minestrone, then salad and bread. The chicken Parmesan was the main course with a side of cheese ravioli.

Throughout the meal, as he served her, his fingers brushed against her with light little touches. Her hand, her wrist. Those little touches sending tingles through her body along with the wine made her feel warmer and warmer.

By the time he cleared the plates and went into the kitchen for the cannoli, she was warm, relaxed, full and happy.

He placed her plate in front of her and then lifted her hair and kissed the back of her neck. "This is the first course of desert and then you get to decide if there will be a second course."

He took her breath away with the kiss, his words, his breath on her neck and the tone of his voice. Every moment of this evening had been perfect.

She looked up at him with complete trust and looking into his eyes, she knew she'd stay for the second course of desert. She would not be calling that taxi for quite some time. She was head over heels in love with Nic and this evening was like a dream.

They moved to the couch and sat beside each other, Jenna feeling shy again, but wanting so much for him to kiss her again. He played with a strand of her hair, his eyes intent upon her and she shivered.

"Are you cold? I can build a fire."

Oh yes you can. The sparks between us are hot enough. Oh, yes. Build up that fire and then take me, right here on this couch.

"Please. I would like that."

He got up and went over to the fireplace. She watched his broad back and firm butt as he squatted down, watched his hands and arms, so strong, muscular and firm. He was the sexiest man she'd ever seen, and soon they'd both be naked. She swallowed hard.

Opening the doors he placed some kindling on the logs and then lit a match and held it while the flame started.

"Eeeeeeeeee!" A sudden woman's shrill scream came from inside the fireplace startling Jenna from her comfortable spot on the couch. "No! No, Nicolo! Stop!"

He stood fast. "What the hell?"

"Oh my God! Is someone in there?" Jenna wrapped her arms around herself suddenly chilled to the bone.

The scream came again. A woman's scream. "Put it out! Are you trying to kill me?"

"There's someone in there!" Incredulous, he grabbed the fire extinguisher and sprayed it on the fire. He yelled, "I put out the fire. You'll be okay. I'm calling the fire department."

"No,' the voice wailed. "Nicolo, I want you to get me out. Only you, Nicolo. Only you."

Jenna stood frozen taking all this in.

Did he know the woman? What was going on? What crazy person would get stuck in a chimney? And why? Why would she be in there in the first place?

"Oh damn. I think I know who she is." He frowned shaking his head and picked up the phone, then dialed and waited.

"No, Nicolo! Don't call them! I want you to get me out!" The woman continued screaming in between repeating herself.

She really is crazy and my God the screaming. The fire is out and the fire department will be on their way soon. Can't she stop screaming? This is crazy.

Jenna wanted to put her hands over her ears to block the woman out though she knew that would do little good as loud as the woman was. She sat in stunned silence as she watched Nicolo making the phone call.

"Hello. I need to report a woman stuck in my chimney. She may be hurt. I started to light a fire but I put it out when I heard the screaming. If she's who I think she is, we need the police." He listened and then gave his address.

The scream came again and Jenna shivered.

To be stuck in a chimney when it was cold and snowing and then the risk of fire. The woman had to be crazy. How did that woman get in there? She'd have to climb down. But why would she climb down Nicolo's chimney? None of this made any sense.

I hope whoever she is; I hope she is all right. If it's who he thinks it is, he said. Does he know the woman?

"Nicolo, do you know that woman?"

"If she's who I think she is, then yes."

"Why would she be in your chimney?"

"It makes no sense." He shook his head. "If that's Ember who is stuck, well she really needs psychiatric care."

"I would think so. Whoever is stuck in there needs it. How will they get her out?"

"That's a good question. I hope the fire department will know what to do."

The wail came again. "Nicolo!"

He went over to the fireplace again and shouted up, "Ember, is that you?"

"Yes," she wailed. "Why did you try to burn me? I love you!"

He rolled his eyes and groaned. "It's her."

"Who is "she"? Ex wife? Ex fiancé? Ex girlfriend?"

She'd better be an ex something. More than that I cannot handle. Not if we are dating. This is far too much crazy making drama going on for me.

"We went on one date. Then she decided she was in love with me and she's been a little obsessed."

"A little? You think? Nicolo, this is more than a little!"

"Yes, I am aware of that and I am taking care of it."

"Okay. Well, I hope they get here soon and get her out."

He came over to her and took her hands in his. "Jenna, I am so sorry this has ruined our evening. This was beyond my control. I had no idea she'd do this. I'll understand if you want to go, but I'd like you to stay."

"Oh, I couldn't tear myself away now. I have to stay and see how this plays out. How they get her out of the chimney and..." she paused searching his eyes, "what happens next."

"What happens next, I hope, is they take her away for medical and pysch evaluation and you forgive me and we try again with our dinner date."

Jenna gave him a hesitant smile. "Well, I would like that too, but lets just see how it goes."

"Yes, of course." Nicolo led her to the couch, to sit and then once she sat, his hands squeezed hers and he said, "Stay."

She nodded her compliance and leaned back on the couch with a sigh and he let loose of her hands. He draped a couch throw around her shoulders and tucked it there with a smile. "I'm going to go get one of my sweatshirts for you to wear and you can wear it home. It's cold out."

"Thank you, Nicolo. I wouldn't want to be dressed like this when the firemen and policemen arrive."

"I know. Sit tight. I'll be right back."

"Nicolo!" the woman in the chimney wailed again.

"Just ignore her. I will handle her."

"Okay."

Though it is not so easy to ignore her. Between the screaming and the wailing. And she's stuck in a chimney? How do you ignore someone who is stuck in a chimney? Oh dear God. This is without doubt the strangest date I have ever been on. One woman in the chimney and the other tucked in on the couch, waiting. Is this normal for Nic? Is he like Chyna said and will there be women, past dates and old exes popping out of the woodwork? Literally in this case. Popping out of a chimney. This is unreal. Oh my God. Is this normal in the life of an actor? And if so, why am I dating one? Even if he is handsome and charming. Women falling out of the woodwork, getting stuck in chimneys, this is a bit too much for me.

She sat on the couch with the couch throw wrapped around her, frowning until something occurred to her.

What a story this would make! What drives a woman to do that? How will Nicolo handle that woman? Even if I decide I never want to go out with him again, this is too fascinating to walk away from. What a story.

And Jenna was a sucker for stories of any kind. With those thoughts, Jenna was now in author observer mode. No longer caught up in the romance of Nicolo and their romantic date turned twilight zone. Her imagination had kicked in, so she was no longer fully present there with Nicolo. She now had the distance of an observer, taking everything in. And she would stay until the last police car and fire truck rolled away.

Nicolo came into the room carrying a dark blue sweatshirt. "It might be a little bit big on you, but you can roll the sleeves."

"Yes, I will have to." She took the sweatshirt he handed her. "Thank you, Nic."

"You're quite welcome." He watched as she let the couch throw drop and then pulled the sweatshirt over her head.

She gave him a smile. "It's soft and warm. It's perfect."

"I don't want you to get cold."

"Nicolo!" the woman screamed. "What about me? I am cold and it's snowing. I'm going to freeze in here. Stop playing with your bimbo and get me out. I'm going to die in here!" She started sobbing. "I thought you loved me but you just want me to die. That's why I'm stuck in this chimney."

Oh dear God, she really is nuts. He dated a lunatic.

"Ember, I want you to calm down. The fire department is on their way. We're going to get you out."

"You just want me to die," she continued to sob. "I know you do."

"I do not want you to die. I want you to get help." He ran his hand through his hair and started to pace.

"It's hard to reason with a crazy person," Jenna said.

"Tell me about it." He looked out the window.

They could hear the sirens blaring as the fire truck neared.

He paced back over to the fireplace and shouted. "Hear that Ember? They are almost here."

The fire truck arrived with sirens blaring and lights flashing. They pulled up in front of the house. Nicolo grabbed his coat, pulled it on and went out to meet them.

Jenna waited till he was outside to bundle up and go out to join him. She was not going to be told to stay inside. She wanted to know what was going to happen next.

"How will you get her out?" Nic was asking the fire chief.

"First we'll try running soapy water down the chimney and send ropes down. Try to pull her out. If that doesn't work, we'll try a sledgehammer and make a hole large enough to get her out. That would destroy your chimney so we'll try the soap first."

"I don't care about the damn chimney. Just get her out safely. Do whatever is best for her."

The fire chief nodded. "Will do."

Jenna watched as they placed ladders up against the house and focused lights to help them see before climbing up. They set up lights above the chimney so they could look down into it and they were trying to talk to the woman who continued to cry for Nicolo.

Soon they poured soapy water down the sides of the chimney and tried to pull the woman out with ropes but she was stuck fast. She did have air to breathe and there was no fire so they attempted to get her out this way several times.

The police had arrived and an officer was now taking a statement from Nicolo.

"We went out once and it became clear that she had some issues to work on." He shook his head. "I told her it wasn't going to work out and suggested she get some help, but she won't listen to me."

"There was a woman out in California, tried the same thing. They met online and went out a few times. But he wasn't a celebrity."

"Did they get that other woman out in time?"

"Yes. Then she was in the psych ward for a while. Have you ever had a stalker before this one?"

"Women get crushes on me all the time, but none has ever gone this far."

"She's lucky she wasn't killed." The officer shook his head. "And you need to be more careful bringing women to your house before you know them well."

Nic glanced over at Jenna and she smiled at him.

Yeah like me.

They shared an understanding glance and a grin.

The woman began screaming again. "Nicolo! I don't want to die!" she wailed. "Get me out of here!"

He's got a crazy stalker ex-girlfriend and I was the one who insisted on getting a taxi because I wanted to feel more secure. To be safe. I guess both men and women need to be careful.

The policeman was done taking his statement so Nic walked over to her. "Ember is going to be charged, but that will get her in where she can be evaluated and maybe she will get the help she needs now."

"I hope so." She looked back to the rooftop where the firemen had given up trying to pull the woman out after sending the soapy water down. Now they were moving back down the ladders. "So how many other crazy exes do you have? How many obsessed fans?"

"No other crazy exes. No stalkers until this one. My fans can get a little carried away but they're harmless. Some send pictures, offers of marriage, things like that, but nothing to get alarmed about. I handle it."

"I'm not sure I'm up for being the girlfriend of a famous actor who is constantly chased around by women, Nic. I like a quiet, drama free life that is peaceful."

"I promise you this kind of thing has never happened before. And once they take Ember away and get her the help she needs, there won't be any more drama. Just please, be patient. Please don't go. I have to deal with this now, but once this is over..."

Between the woman's screaming and the men's shouting, both of which had gotten louder, Nic and Jenna's attention went to the firemen and both quieted as they watched.

The attempt to pull her out had failed.

The one remaining fireman on top of the roof was fed up. "Enough!" he yelled down at her. "Now you shut up and listen!"

The woman quieted her screaming and wailing.

He yelled down at her. "Okay, ma'am you just hang in there and don't be alarmed. We are going to knock out some bricks so we can free you. We know how to get you out, we just had to try the other way first."

"Get me out," the woman wailed. "Nicolo! Get me out! I don't want to die in here."

"You're not going to die." The fireman shouted down at her. "We're going to get you out. Once I climb down we will start knocking a hole into the chimney to get you out."

"Nicolo," she wailed. "Where is Nicolo? I want Nicolo."

The fireman shook his head and then started down the ladder as Ember continued to wail for Nicolo.

Nic groaned.

"I'll bet you're ready for this night to be over," Jenna said. "And I don't blame you. None of this is your fault. Once they get her out though, I'm going back to the hotel."

"Jenna, I am so sorry about all this." He reached for her but she took a step backward, determined to keep some distance.

And if I let you touch me, I'll be right back on that couch, losing my clothes. Which is not what I need right now. I need to be away from all this. I need to think. I have to go.

There it was again, that urge to run.

I'll call a cab as soon as that woman is safe and then I have to go.

CHAPTER SIX

Nic started to speak and Jenna held up her hand. "Nic, wait. I don't want to talk about this right now. I'm tired and you have a woman to get out of your chimney."

"Jenna, please." He stepped forward, but she stepped backward again and he stopped.

"We…" she frowned, trying to find what she wanted to say and fighting the beginning of a headache brought on by stress, the sirens and the woman screaming. "We can start over and we'll talk about this. Just not tonight. I want to be sure that woman is out safe before I leave but then I just want to go back to my room where it is quiet."

"All right," he said quietly stepping back with a nod. "Tomorrow."

A large man with big meaty hands was now wielding the sledgehammer.

Bang.

Bang.

Bang.

Bricks started to loosen from the mortar that held them together. The loud sounds echoed through the dark night. Lights from one of the trucks were aimed directed at the chimney where the demolition was now taking place.

And TV reporters had pulled up in their news trucks. "Great," Nicolo grumbled. "Just great." He glanced at Jenna. "You might want to stand over there with the neighbors so they don't connect me with you. Unless you want to be interviewed."

"Oh my God, no." She frowned deeper, her head pounding now. "That's the last thing I need right now." She took a deep breath. "Okay, I'll watch from over there. Good night Nic."

"Good night, sweet girl. I'll call you tomorrow."

She nodded and hurried away toward the crowd gathered on the edge of the lawn. Stepping back behind a tall thin older man, she hoped she blended in with the crowd and that they wouldn't notice her.

Jenna stood watching, through the demolition of the chimney, as the TV cameras rolled while the fire chief and Nic were interviewed, and during the final moments when the woman was finally pulled out and reached for Nic screaming. She felt removed from Nicolo, as if she was watching a movie with the distance of the observer. This was his life happening right in front of her and it had nothing to do with her. It was a life she was not sure she wanted any part of.

By the time the woman was taken away in an ambulance, with a policeman riding along beside her, Jenna had a cab there ready to take her back to the hotel. She hurried into it, hoping the TV crew hadn't noticed that she didn't live there and told the cabby to hurry, while praying they wouldn't follow her.

Looking out the back window of the cab she thought, *this is ridiculous. This is not how I want to live my life, hiding from reporters.*

The problem was she was in love with Nic already. There seemed to be no happy answer that wouldn't cause her stress or heart pain.

Her cell phone rang when she was halfway to the hotel.

"Jenna, where are you?" He sounded worried.

"In the cab, almost to my hotel."

"Good." She could hear the relief in his voice. "You disappeared. Once everything was over I looked for you."

"I called a cab and left right when they drove her away in the ambulance."

"I'm glad you are okay. Let me know when you are safe in your room."

"Yes, Nic. I will."

"I'm sorry how our dinner date turned out. I want to make it up to you."

"Nic, I just need a little time and for things to settle down. You can call me tomorrow and we can talk about it then. Now I'm going to go, but I'll message you once I am in my room."

"All right." Nic had grown very quiet.

"It has been a long evening for both of us. Get some rest Nic."

"I will. Sweet dreams, Jenna."

"Thank you, Nic. Night."

"Good night."

The taxi pulled up to the hotel and she got out and paid the man. Then she walked in and asked the front desk to hold any calls until she notified them otherwise. Riding up to her room in the elevator she wanted nothing more than a warm bath and a good long sleep.

Once she closed the door to her room she sent Nic a text message.

"Safe. Good night."

"Good. Sleep well, sweetheart."

She closed her eyes and sighed.

How could she give him up when he was so wonderful to her? How could she continue to see him when his lifestyle was one that she didn't belong in?

There were no good answers.

* * * *

The next day, she slept in very late and when she woke her headache was gone. After ordering room service, she wrote, then ate as she wrote, then wrote some more. Writing was her world and it centered her to be back to it.

In her writing world, good guys always won, bad guys always lost, and her heroines always ended up with the man of their dreams. When she finally stopped writing for the day, she felt better for having written. As if the crazy world from last night that she'd been living in had righted itself.

She turned her phone back on, saw that she had two calls from Nic, but only one message. He'd left it on the second call.

"Hello, Jenna. I hope you slept well last night and that everything is all right. Please call me when you're up."

She called down to the front desk and there were no calls or messages.

Whew, good. The reporters didn't catch on that I was there with Nic. So everything should be all right.

She picked up her phone and called Nic. He answered on the

second ring, with a cheerful voice. "Hello. How are you feeling today?"

"Better. I slept well. Thank you."

"Good. Want to go out for pizza? Or I could bring one there and we could hang out."

Hanging out in my room is not a good idea. Not when we need to talk. Not with the chemistry we have between us.

"I'd rather go out for pizza."

"I know the perfect place. What time should I pick you up?"

"About an hour? I still need to take a shower."

"I'll see you in an hour."

"Okay, see you then." She hung up and went to take her shower. Though she'd had a bath last night, her hair was a tangled mess from tossing and turning all night. She'd not bothered with a comb when she got up. She looked in the mirror and laughed. The room service guy must have thought she looked a sight.

Soon she was ready and Nic was pulling up in his corvette. He got out and offered her the keys. "Want to drive?"

"Seriously?"

"I wouldn't tease you about something like this. I trust you."

Wow. He trusts me to drive his fancy corvette.

"Yes, I'd love to."

He handed her the keys. "You drive and I'll navigate. You're going to like this place. Best pizza in town."

They got in the car and her nerves kicked in.

"Just relax Jenna. Take your time. Nothing to be nervous about. It's just a car."

Just a car, he says. When I know this is his baby. I see the way he treats her and I know how men are about their fancy cars.

She took a deep breath and then adjusted the seat and the rear view mirror for her shorter stature. She pulled away from the curb. "Which way?"

"Turn left and keep going until I tell you."

"Okay."

The drive was quiet, with her paying attention to the car, the road and his directions. They reached the restaurant and she parked and handed him the keys.

"Nice job."

"Thanks for letting me drive her."

"You're welcome. Did you have fun?"

"Yes, I did."

"Good. Come on." He got out of the car and she did as well. "You're going to love their pizza."

Somehow she felt they were now in a friendship pattern, not a dating pattern. He hadn't opened doors for her and he'd let her drive. He was friendly and relaxed like he'd been the day they watched football in his room. She wasn't getting the feeling this was like a date, at all.

He did hold the door to the restaurant for her and she walked in, wondering if she was wrong about that. Everything was so confusing now. She didn't know what to think. Yet another reason they needed to talk.

Inside, the tables were covered with red and white checked plastic tablecloths. Parmesan cheese and red pepper shakers stood on the tables along with napkin holders that held white napkins. They sat and looked at the menu behind the counter.

Both agreed the super veggie pizza was the one they wanted. Their waitress came and took their order and when she left, Jenna wasn't sure how to begin or what to say.

"Jenna, I want to tell you again how sorry I am about what happened last night."

"Nic, please, don't apologize. You couldn't have known what that crazy woman would do."

"I hate that she ruined our evening."

"Me too. It was a lovely evening before that happened. Dinner was delicious. You're a very good cook."

"I enjoy cooking."

"It shows."

The waitress brought their drinks and when she walked away Jenna picked up her straw and unwrapped it. She slipped it into her drink and then sat toying with the wrapper. "I've been thinking. The lifestyle you live, it isn't one that has room for someone like me."

"What do you mean? Of course I have room for you."

"I mean the reporters, the fans, the girls chasing you around. I just don't fit into all that. I don't want to live a Hollywood lifestyle."

"You think I live a Hollywood lifestyle? You have noticed my house is in New Jersey, right?"

"Well, this one. I thought you said you had a place in LA."

"I do. But this is my home. Where my family lives. I stay out there when I am working."

"Oh. But the women..."

"How many women have you seen chasing me around since you got here? There's just the one and she's undergoing psychiatric care now."

"I was going to ask you how she was."

"She's fine and you're changing the subject."

The pizza came and she smiled at the waitress who had also brought two plates.

"Saved by the pizza. You're going to love it."

Jenna laughed. "Saved by the pizza." She reached for a slice and took a bite. "Mmm. This is good."

Nic grinned. "Enjoy."

They ate for a few moments in silence and then he said, "So. You're still coming to Christmas dinner with us, I hope."

"Yes, Nic. If you still want me to."

"Silly girl, of course I do! We want you to come."

"Okay, good. Because I've been looking forward to it."

"All right. That's settled." He smiled at her. "Now about us dating..."

"Yes, we should talk about that."

"You said we could start over."

"I did say that." she nodded.

"Jenna Heart, I would like to take you out. I'm glad we are friends, but what I really want is for you to be my girlfriend."

"Your girlfriend. What would that mean? Would you be dating other women? Will I be the Friday night girlfriend?"

He cocked his head and looked at her. "You can't seriously think I would treat a woman like that. That I would treat my girl like that?"

"Well, I don't know, Nic. We've only been out once and then in at your house once. I'm confused and I don't know what to think."

"When I date a woman, she doesn't have to compete with anyone. There are no girlfriends looking for catfights, there is no drama like there was last night. I don't know how to get this through to you."

"So you only date one woman at a time?"

"Yes."

"Oh. Good."

"Jenna, my life is my work, the time I spend with the kids visiting them in the hospital and at home, and my family. I like to travel and often I take my girl with me, but there is no drama. There's just fun and spending time together. Now. Do you think you can handle my lifestyle?"

"Yes."

"Then, will you be my girl?"

"Yes, Nic." she beamed.

"Good! Because this being just friends is hard to get used to when all I want to do right now is kiss you." He reached with his finger and brushed her bottom lip.

Her lips parted and she felt them tingle.

"Pizza sauce," he said. "I'd much rather have kissed that off. You're my dream woman, you know. Even taste like pizza. I could eat you up right now."

There it was. That sexual chemistry between them and the sudden urge she had to start losing her clothes again.

Her cheeks heated at the thoughts she was now having. "We could go back to my room."

"Or my place," he said.

"Oh yes, let's go." Suddenly she was in a hurry. There were only a few more days left on this trip and they'd already used up so much time.

They got a box for the pizza and as they left he said, "This time I'll drive."

He helped her into the car and then got in. "You sit back and relax." He turned soft music on and they rode in silence, his hand on her leg in between handling the wheel. The heat from his hand warming her up inside.

At his house, he parked and they got out. The damage from the previous night to the chimney had left a huge hole but it did not extend into the other side of the chimney so the house was secured against weather. "I'll repair it soon," he said. "Have put the call in and they'll start on it after the holidays."

"Oh good. I'm glad there's not more damage. It's bad enough but at least the weather can't get in."

He unlocked the house and picked up the mail from the floor.

There was a card on top. The envelope was covered with red lipstick prints.

"What is that?" Jenna frowned.

Not again. Not more crazy. He said there was no more crazy.

"It's nothing." He crumpled it up and went to throw it in the trash.

"It's from that woman isn't it? Or is there another one out there?"

"I told you there wasn't. That's Ember's handwriting."

"You threw it away. Isn't that evidence?"

"It would be if I were taking her to court. But climbing down my chimney is evidence enough that she needs psychiatric help. She's been charged with breaking and entering and they have her in the psych ward right now. Apparently she had a break down before all the paperwork was even processed. She must have mailed this before she came here last night."

Jenna had tensed up again.

He came up to her and put his hands on her shoulders. Looking down into her eyes he said, "Do you trust me? Because this is only going to work if you trust me."

"Yes, Nic. I trust you."

"It wasn't sounding like it a minute ago. There are no secrets here Jenna. I promise. I just need you to trust me."

"I do."

"Come on," he said. "I'll put on a movie, we can cuddle on the couch and you can relax. There's no pressure here, no stress. Just you and me relaxing. Think you can handle that?"

"Yes, Nic. That sounds nice. Real nice."

"All right then."

They went into the living room and he placed a DVD in and then came to sit on the couch next to her and hit play on the remote.

Romancing the Stone came on.

"Oh, that's one of my favorites," she said.

"I thought you would like that," he said with a grin then he opened his arms to her, "now come here."

She snuggled up next to him and they started to watch the show.

* * * *

On Christmas Eve snow was falling and Jenna was more filled with Christmas spirit than she'd ever been in her life.

She'd been floating on a happy cloud ever since she'd spent the night with Nic two nights ago. Though they hadn't progressed past oral sex yet, he made her feel so loved and desired she couldn't imagine being happier than she was tonight. He was taking things slow with her and wooing her with every little thing he did.

Just like the heroes in her books, but even better, because he was Nic.

Nic helped her off with her coat and hung it in the closet. "Mom, we're here." he called toward the kitchen as her reached for Jenna's hand. "Come on. She'll be in the kitchen."

The scents coming from the kitchen were fantastic. Garlic, onions, homemade sauces, pastas. Nic was right; his mother had prepared a feast.

"Welcome, Jenna! I'm glad you could join us," Angela said. She rinsed off her hands, dried them and then came forward to give Jenna a hug.

Jenna hugged her back thinking how lucky Nic was to have a mom like her.

"Would you like some eggnog?" Angela asked. "We have regular spiced with rum and also non alcoholic eggnog for the kids."

"Yes, I'd love some."

Nic fixed her a cup and handed it to her so his mom could get back to the dinner preparations.

"Thank you."

Jenna took the cup from him and took a sip. She could taste the rum in it and the nutmeg. Everything in the kitchen smelled so good, the familiar scent and taste of the eggnog making her feel at home. "It's delicious. Mother always made eggnog for Christmas."

"I know," Angela winked. "Nic told me."

"Oh, he did?" Jenna looked and Nic who just smiled.

The entire Maldini family came for dinner and Jenna was surrounded by and welcomed into their warm, talkative, affectionate fold.

During dinner Jenna was telling Nic's sister that at first she just couldn't believe Nic had any interest in her as a girlfriend.

Nic interrupted her. "I like a girl who is family oriented. Affectionate. Caring and giving. Selfless. So, of course, Jenna caught my eye right away."

They cleared away the dinner dishes and then Nic pulled her aside and said, "We're going to watch It's A Wonderful Life."

"We are? Oh, I would love that." Then she remembered she'd told him all about the things she used to do with her mother at Christmas such as drinking eggnog and watching It's a Wonderful Life every year. "I know what you're doing."

"What? What am I doing?" He turned on the TV and patted the couch beside him. "Come over here. I won't bite." he grinned.

"Much."

Jenna giggled remembering the night they'd spent together and knew she was turning pink again. She sat on the couch next to him.

He curled his left arm around her and picking up the remote, started the movie. She curled in beside him to watch, allowing his warmth and strength to keep her company.

Of course memories of all the years she had watched it with her mother came back to her and there were tears, but with this movie, there always were. Nicolo seemed to know just when she needed a squeeze and his loving support meant more to her than she could have said.

When Chyna had said I have to stop being so damn helpful she was wrong. I like helping people and giving makes me happy. I am a giver and Nicolo is a giver and when two givers meet and fall in love it is a wonderful thing.

She'd wished for one thing from Santa this Christmas. She'd wished to spend Christmas with someone who wanted her there, so she wouldn't spend Christmas alone. Santa had done more than grant her wish and she suspected her guardian angel had a hand in this Christmas gift too.

She closed her eyes and whispered, "Thank you for answering my Christmas wish and my prayers."

When she opened her eyes Nicolo was looking right at her. He threaded his fingers through hers and said, "I'm thankful God led me to you."

"I'm thankful you found me too."

"Jenna, you are my wish come true."

Her breath caught. Nicolo wasn't just her wish come true, she was his wish come true too. Her thankful list would be very full tonight. And tonight she would make sure another wish Nic surely had would come true.

She would be her St. Nic's Christmas gift tonight. She planned to wear a Santa hat and nothing else. Tonight she would give herself to him in every way; he just didn't know it yet. A small smile crossed her lips.

He bent to kiss her and as her eyes closed and their lips touched she knew this was home. With Nic, she was home.

I'll be home for Christmas, the song played.

Home. I already am home. Right here in his arms. There's no place I'd rather be.

THE END

62241062R00070

Made in the USA
Charleston, SC
04 October 2016